Publish and be damned
www.pabd.com

Wold

Paul Judges

Publish and be damned
www.pabd.com

First published in Great Britain 2004 by Paul Judges.
The moral right of Paul Judges to be identified as the author of this work has
been asserted.

Designed in London, Great Britain, by Adlibbed Limited.
Printed and bound in the UK.

This novel is a work of fiction and the characters and events in it
exist only in its pages and in the imagination of the author.

ISBN: 1-905059-55-8

To my family

No wonder young Jeff was grumpy - he was supposed to be marrying Ethel, but for months had to endure living with the peculiar chaps at Wold House.

He found sleep particularly difficult, always expecting a knock on the door:

"Are you awake Jeff ?".

He would pretend to be snoring; then listen to the owls, or foxes bark, sensing Mars grow bigger and nearer on the other side of the Wold.

Jeff thought about Et in the next village, lying naked on her single bed, wishing they could be together sooner. How could he survive week after week with these chubby, bald, middle-aged men ?

1

At dawn he quietly left Wold House, taking the muddy lane by the clear, chalk beck, steadily climbing up the Wold. It was such a relief to be outside, away from friendly landlord and the landlord's close friend.

Jeff found himself walking towards her house, hoping that he could slip in the back door and upstairs without parents noticing. His mind was filled with the sharp, blue morning sky and Ethel's lovely, firm breasts.

He could see the red-tiled roofs of her village, and even though it was August some of the cottages had smoke rising from chimneys. How peaceful and inviting it looked; and how the hell had he become stuck with two blokes so unlike himself?

It had seemed a good offer at the time - Jeff didn't get on with his mum and dad, and the men he'd just met at the Little Angel pub were a good laugh:

"Stay with us if you like".

"I don't know you ".

"We've got plenty of room".

Jeff had consumed a few pints of Waggledick, and couldn't face another argument with his dad.

"Just for tonight then".

He hadn't realised that the two chaps were casting their eyes over his young body, as if it were a fine piece of pottery. Jeff had been too busy eyeing-up the barmaid, who was looking better and better as the beer flowed.

He liked the Little Angel - a good atmosphere, particularly on Saturday night - and not too many serious punch-ups. He'd met Ethel there a few years before and after a couple of weeks they'd gone to the Palace to see some crap Hollywood blockbuster. Outside they started kissing, and now they wanted to get married.

He opened Ethel's back door, the kitchen was warm and quiet - everybody still asleep. Jeff knew exactly which stairs not to step on, it wouldn't be a good idea to wake her dad, who was a miserable old git at the best of times.

Ethel turned towards him in the single bed, she was used to the surprise visits. Jeff admired her slim body in the strong morning light. He quickly removed t-shirt and jeans, and they held each other in the passion that sustained and consumed. Even though their relationship had lasted a long time compared with friends locally, neither tired of the regular sexual feeding frenzy.

Ethel woke a few hours later, knowing that the house would be deserted except for them.

"Jeff " she nudged him in the ribs.

"What ?".

"I'll make a picnic and we can go to the springs near Millington".

"Excellent ! I fancy a splash where the Roman road crosses".

2

Jeff loved to sit by the clear spring water that bubbled endlessly from the chalk wolds, imagining Roman soldiers halting for a 'tea-break' then marching on towards Malton or York. He was amazed by the thousands of springs spurting out all over the place, swelling into becks, streams, rivers. Often he would wander about alone, but today he was with Ethel.

"Lovely and warm now", she said.

"Get your kit off then !".

"Don't you ever give it a rest ?!".

"Never".

Jeff couldn't envisage a day when their passion would dwindle, and maybe it wouldn't; but he had little time for reality, choosing whenever possible to inhabit a world removed from work and ordinary life.

"Do you want a Marmite sarnie ?".

"Have you got any cheese ?".

"No. What about ham ?".

"Give me Marmite then".

There were very few people around the shallow beck crossing that could hardly have changed for thousands of years. Occasionally a farm vehicle would thunder past on the tiny road above, but that was it. Jeff knew that people had seen ghosts of Roman soldiers, and he could almost feel them as their only companions in the grassy, chalk valley.

Et was paddling close to the long wooden bridge, and Jeff watched her careful steps through the water, admiring those long legs, and then the familiar breasts as she leant forward to peer into the stream. He had no idea how he could cope without the infectious laugh that had become part of daily routine.

"Come on in then !"

"Right !".

He ripped off his trainers and ran towards her, splashing and shouting.

"Shut up you noisy sod".

"There's nobody here but us".

"I thought you believed in the ghosts ?".

"Not so much on a hot, bright day like this. Maybe on a grey, winter afternoon".

Ethel pulled him towards her, and they kissed tenderly, causing consternation amongst the lapwings and legionnaires.

3

"Where have you been ?" , asked Roger, his landlord.

"Keeping away from you benders".

"What I do with Paul in the privacy of this house is our affair".

"Fair enough", Jeff grudgingly admitted.

"Can you help me lay some slabs out the back ?".

"OK".

"There's a few pints in it for you".

Even if Jeff didn't much like Roger and Paul, he couldn't deny that they were both generous with cash. He also knew that a few pints actually meant fifty or sixty quid for a couple of hours work - not bad for someone without a job. A chance to give Et a treat; or just get pissed at the pub.

Jeff had been offered work at the Little Angel, but Et wasn't sure if it was a good idea considering his track record with strong ale. She didn't want him getting too friendly with that slag of a barmaid either.

Et was hoping they'd be able to 'babysit' a relative's cottage - it was very run down, but they wouldn't have to pay much in rent. She didn't mind keeping Jeff for a while, as long as he brought some money from odd jobs, and she kept on working at the big hotel. They both were coming to realise that marriage might be a way off, but nothing could stop them living together at Beck Cottage.

"Pass me that big one Jeff".

"Bloody Hell ! What are they made of ?".

"York stone. Don't make a fuss ! I thought you were a real man".

"More than you'll ever be".

"I don't know. I'd expect today's youth to have more positive views about same sex relationships".

"Bollocks".

Roger and Jeff worked hard through the hot afternoon, not saying a great deal to each other. They didn't have much in common, or that was what Jeff was determined to prove. Even when they stopped for a couple of cold lagers Jeff wasn't keen to talk, he didn't want to admit that deep down he actually preferred Roger to his own dad.

"Do you fancy a few jars tonight then ?".

"Depends what Et is doing".

"I haven't seen her recently".

Jeff didn't respond. He sipped the lager, thinking of the lady that made his life worthwhile. It would be late when she finished work, and he wasn't sure if she'd make the pub before closing - or maybe for yet another lock-in.

The Police would either turn a blind-eye to the after hours drinking at the Little Angel, or take an active part in the regular beer-swilling contests. Most locals believed that if you could drink at 8pm then why not 2am the next morning ? Fortunately, the PC who lived in the village really liked his ale, even though he was an arrogant bastard who'd seen too many Westerns where a powerful Sheriff cleans up a lawless town.

Jeff wasn't particularly keen on the Police - he realised they could do plenty of good, but were also bound to act as tools of oppression - as in the miners' strike led by Arthur Scargill, when that evil bitch Thatcher used them so cruelly to uphold 'the law'. He didn't get on with his dad, but he had taught him to love ordinary people and despise injustice.

Luckily, his area of the Wolds was far removed from industrial unrest - sure it had many problems, but brutal policing wasn't one of them.

4

On a warm night in early summer Jeff had slept on the prehistoric burial mounds on the Wold. God knows why, because even warm nights tended to be a bit chilly up there on the chalk. He'd taken a sleeping bag, a flask of coffee and some pork pies, determined to commune with nature and meet the ancestors.

He knew absolutely nothing about the historical background, but felt in some way ancient people would make themselves known - whether through dreams or something more tangible like finding artefacts.

"You're fucking crazy !", Ethel had said.

"I'll fuck you crazy if you come with me".

"You wouldn't catch me up there, even in daylight".

"What are you scared of ?".

"Just the cold, and flints sticking in my arse".

"I think I can really find something".

"You're talking shite".

"You won't say that when I come back with a sword or coins".

"The only thing you'll come back with is frozen toes !".

The reality of the night was uncomfortable and mostly sleepless, waking up to a sleeping bag soggy with dew. He looked down over the misty vale, munching a last pork pie and sipping cold coffee. Jeff had seen pheasants, rabbits and hares, but nothing that might really kindle the imagination and stop Et sneering.

Whatever was said he knew something was out there, and one day they'd introduce themselves - when time warped or his mind warped, or both.

It felt good to walk back through the empty fields, eventually coming to the little beck gurgling and rushing towards the village. He couldn't wait to get into a warm bed and dream what hadn't happened.

Et was waiting at the gate that led from fields into the dark lane enclosed by trees.

"Didn't think you'd be up yet".

"Thought it'd be nice to meet you. You're looking a bit rough!".

Et pulled him close, kissing tenderly.

"That's a nice welcome. I was going back to mine, but maybe you can do me a fry-up ?".

"We'll have to wait a while till the folks go to work".

"It's warming up now, so we can sit here and listen to the water".

5

Jeff had become good friends with Pete, the landlord of the Little Angel. This was mainly because Jeff had listened to Pete's sad tales about the loss of his soul mate - a girl courted more than twenty years before in the delightful surroundings of Leeds. Jeff had been sworn to secrecy, as there was no way Pete wanted his wife to know he still loved this mystery lady.

Pete acknowledged it was all hopeless, as he had kids and he knew that she did, and it would be impossible for them to get together unless their partners died !

He'd actually fancied her friend first, but she was going out with some bearded fop, so almost by accident Pete ended up talking to Jane, who wanted to finish with her lightweight chap. Both lovers were nineteen with little experience, but it didn't take long for them to become very close.

Pete's wife went to Tai Chi classes twice a week, so this gave him chance to pour his heart out, and pour Jeff several free pints into the bargain. It wasn't that he didn't love his wife and kids, but what had been lost still caused pain after all this time.

"Got any pork scratchings Pete ? This beer's a bit wet on its own".

"You greedy little sod".

"I'm still growing - upwards, not outwards like you !".

"You won't be laughing when you get to my age".

"I might be if I'm in charge of all this booze".

"It's no picnic running a pub".

Both were silent for a minute, then Jeff asked:

"So what did she look like, this Jane ?".

"Tall, dark, not too thin, nice little breasts, lovely arse, lovely big eyes".

"Sounds alright mate".

"She certainly was, or is - I imagine. Probably wouldn't want anything to do with me now - fat and bald ain't too inspiring".

"Maybe you're right", Jeff said unsympathetically.

"But I'm still the same person inside ! And I'm still mad for her".

Pete went all sad and quiet, and Jeff felt a little uncomfortable.

"I'll put some more logs on that fire".

Jeff sipped his pint. As the flames began to lick the slightly damp wood he thought about Pete's story, wondering how things would turn out with Et.

Pete had said how difficult their first dates had been - Jane nearly gave up on him immediately because he hardly said a word on those first summer walks. Their main form of communication became sex, because it was hard at first knowing what to say. Much to Pete's dismay Jane had complained that they did it too much ! She thought they ought to go shopping together, or see a film with another couple.

If only they'd both been older, Pete was sure things could have become permanent, but he hadn't known himself well enough, let alone her. This made Jeff doubt his own relationship even more - how could it survive ? He didn't have a job, a home, just a passion similar to that still burning in the middle-aged landlord, despite all his wasted years.

6

Ethel was moved by Jeff's latest recounting of the lost love in Pete's life. She was tired of seemingly endless shifts at the hotel, clearing up after ungrateful guests, and was feeling a little emotional.

"Do you think we can survive ?".

"We love each other", reassured Jeff.

"But so did Pete and that woman".

"We're young, but it's like we understand each other without trying. I think we'll stay together".

"So do I".

The young lovers held each other in the lounge of Wold House. Roger and Paul had gone to Stratford for the weekend to see Shakespeare.

"I thought Shakespeare was dead", said Jeff.

"Very amusing. You know very well they're seeing a play".

"I bet those two puffs wouldn't mind dressing-up as girls".

"You're such a tolerant person Jeff !".

"That's why you love me".

"I suppose I do".

"What do you mean suppose ? You won't do better round here; do you really want to shag a young farmer ?".

"Shut up and give us a kiss".

"Fetch me a beer luv".

"I've been bloody working !".

"OK keep your hair on, I'll do the honours - might even bring some crisps as well".

"Got any dips ?"

"What do you think this is, a bloody hotel ?!".

Jeff went off to the kitchen, and Et smiled to herself, knowing that despite his faults she loved the silly sod very much.

She started to look through Roger and Paul's video collection, which appeared to be somewhat outside the normal range. The first one Et selected had a picture of a Nazi on the front holding an enormous bratwurst, most of the words on the box were in German but under the title it said in English: (My sausage is swollen !).

"We're not watching any of that !", said Jeff returning with refreshments.

"It's not exactly Disney family viewing is it ?".

"Bloody perverts those two".

"They've been good to you".

"Maybe. But how long till we can move into Beck Cottage ?".

"Could be next month if we can get those few roof tiles fixed".

"Our own place at last, it'll be fantastic".

"No more dodging parents".

"Endless sex !".

"You'll be too busy with DIY".

"We don't want to end up like all the other couples, washing the car on Sunday".

"Don't worry".

They settled back together on the couch - it wasn't long before an exhausted Et was snoring, and Jeff struggled hard to keep his eyes open.

7

When the landlady of the Little Angel realised that her partner was deeply in love with another woman her pubic hair turned white overnight. The same thing had happened to her mother when daddy ran off with the milkman in 1965.

With so many fine hair care products on the market it was no longer necessary for a lady to live with this affliction, so Julie went straight to Boots for a remedy. Pete probably wouldn't have noticed anyway as he was so wrapped-up in dreamy delusions.

Julie soon returned to her natural ginger. She was determined not to reveal her unhappy knowledge of the 'affair' to the man she still loved, and was convinced that sooner or later he'd come to his senses, realising that the pub and family life were pretty good.

She went to the Ann Summers shop in the big town and picked out some crotchless panties with matching bra that allowed nipples to poke through 'like chapel hat pegs'. Julie was convinced that any man could not turn his nose-up at sex, and of course this is normally true. Pete however might prove more of a challenge, as he was so very lost in unreality.

"I never thought we'd get the place shut tonight", said Pete wearily.

"Not to worry, you come and snuggle up here".

"Blimey, what have you got on ?".

"Nothing special".

Pete could feel his bratwurst swelling, as the bedside light gently illuminated Julie's partially dressed body. Despite the months of wallowing in the past it didn't take him long to be fully involved in the moment. She began to feel that everything might turn out OK.

At first he'd been put off by seeing her sprawled on the bed - 'piss flaps like a torn welly' as a former colleague had so charmingly put it. But Julie had been right about the simple motives that drive a lusty male, however romantic they might claim to be. And Pete did love Julie in the everyday way that is enough for most people in this life dominated by shopping and anything superficial.

When their lovemaking was complete she held him very tightly, as if this might stop his body and mind straying forever. Deep down Julie knew that he was a dreamer who'd never let go of a fanciful love from years ago, but she was determined to be his reality - the family would stick together no matter what.

8

It was mid-September when the young lovers moved into Beck Cottage, to nest under the patched-up roof. The day was chilly but bright, and the tiny beck that had depleted over the dry summer gently washed over chalk. They didn't have much stuff, but in an unusually generous gesture Jeff's dad had bought them a new double bed.

Et and Jeff were both exhilarated at finally getting their own place, even if the house loan wasn't to be a long-term thing; there weren't many youngsters round about who'd flown the parental prison.

"What do you think ?", asked Et, who had spent the last few weeks knocking the cottage into shape.

"Great".

"It is".

There wasn't much either felt like saying, rather succumbing to the general feeling of unadulterated joy. Jeff slammed the front door, and they raced up the short stairs to a new, pine bed.

"I've always said my dad was a fine fellow !".

"Lying bastard !".

"We don't need to worry now".

They made love with the usual tender ferocity, falling asleep as the afternoon warmed their small world a little more. The beck had soothed them into dreams - the spring-fed water that never failed.

It wasn't long before Jeff heard the low roar of his mate's large Triumph motorbike.

"Quick Et, get dressed Dave's here".

"Bloody hell !".

They both struggled into jeans and t-shirts, and Jeff dashed down to open the door.

"What have you been doing ?", Dave grinned.

"None of your business you tosser, get inside".

"Where's the Mrs ?".

"She'll be down in a minute. Do you fancy a beer ?".

"Not when I'm on the bike. Maybe see you down the pub tonight ?".

Jeff didn't answer because he knew Et was planning a special meal to celebrate moving in.

"I can't see *your* lady friend", said Jeff.

"That bitch has gone off with some bloke on a massive Suzuki".

"I'm not surprised - that knackered machine of yours".

"It's a bloody classic !".

Ethel came downstairs, and the boys shut up for a moment.

"I hope you two aren't falling out again".

"Just a friendly discussion", said Jeff.

"I'll make some tea, if I can get the cooker going".

"It's alright Et, I just came to see if your man was coming to the Little Angel tonight".

"If *we* do it'll be around last orders".

Dave wasn't too comfortable with domestic bliss, and made a hasty retreat to the familiar saddle of his classic bike.

"You Jeffrey, can stay in and suffer my cooking", Et joked.

"I wouldn't want anything else darling".

The afternoon turned grey and cold, giving Jeff the perfect opportunity to light their first fire. Central heating could undoubtedly give you a warm house, but there was no substitute for the real thing. First the logs got going, then he added a small amount of house coal that sent black smoke up the chimney.

"This is what it's all about. Get us some beers Et".

"Coming".

They curled up on the old couch like two contented cats, watching flames grow taller in the hearth and dancing shadows on the low ceiling.

It wasn't long before there was another knock at the door, and Et got up to have a peek from behind a partially open curtain.

"It's Roger and Paul".

"Not those two puffs !".

"Don't be ridiculous, I'll invite them in".

Despite Jeff's attitude, Et liked them very much; and here they were laden with all sorts of delights - champagne, a brace of pheasant, a painting of the village by a local artist, and a selection of cheese.

"Jeff doesn't deserve this, not with the things he says about you".

"We're still fond of him - well both of you".

"Thanks", managed Jeff reluctantly.

"How are you settling in ?", Paul asked.

"Very quickly, it's fantastic !", beamed Et.

"I'll get some beer".

Jeff went to the kitchen, leaving the three of them chatting in front of a blazing fire.

"That's rather hot !", Roger said, wiping sweat from his brow.

"Wish we had a real fire", Paul chipped in.

"Who'd clean it out ?".

"Good point", agreed Paul.

Jeff returned with drinks, while Roger began a long tale about first setting-up home with Paul many years before, and the very mixed reaction of locals to their gay marriage.

"The vicar said it was unnatural".

"He did !", agreed Paul.

"The postmistress was nice about it".

"Yes, she was".

"What about Lord Fimber though ?".

"He's just a bastard", Jeff said with venom.

"Most folk would agree with you", said Paul.

All four burst out laughing, and Jeff found himself enjoying the company of his former landlords. It was getting dark, the flames had died a little, beer and chat flowed freely in the cosy lounge.

"I had a run-in with his hunt last year", Jeff said bitterly.

"I can't understand why people still consider it a sport in the 21st century", replied Et.

Roger spoke for both of them: "We're no fan of ripping foxes to shreds either".

"There's some bloody mental midgets in the countryside", Jeff complained. "Haven't they heard of computer games ?".

"Anyway, let's not get too depressed, it's supposed to be your happy day". Roger tried to lighten the mood.

"It's our happiest day", Et smiled.

9

Because of the financial pressures that come with independent living, Jeff had been forced into the extraordinary position of getting a job. He'd realised that unless action was taken Et would never shut up about it (despite her more relaxed attitude before the move). He hoped that the part-time position secured through a friend in the local council offices would be less demanding than working for a real business.

Jeff wasn't too worried as one of his better school subjects had been computing, and virtually all office work is now on a PC.

"It must get confusing for the Police".

"Why ?", Et replied.

"A PC working on a PC".

"Is that supposed to be funny ?".

"No, not really".

"According to you, I thought the role of Police is to mercilessly beat-up the poor and oppressed".

"They have to use computers now as well".

Jeff didn't think he'd last long at the council, because he hated being told what to do. Within a few weeks he expected to be spending lazy days wandering the hills again.

"You be good, we need the extra cash".

"I'll do my best".

"It shouldn't be too bad - only 20 hours".

"Suppose so".

It was six miles to the nearest town and new place of work, but fortunately Jeff had borrowed a 125cc scooter from his mate Dave. There was no bus, and no way he would cycle the hilly twelve miles there and back.

"Watch yourself on that bike as well".

"Do stop fussing".

"Well, it's not exactly the safest mode of transport".

"I'll go slowly. I'm not one of those nutters riding on the wrong side of the road at over a 100 mph".

"It's the mad farmers in their Land Rovers you've got to watch".

Jeff enjoyed a careful ride into town, and arrived at the modern offices in a happy frame of mind. He didn't see why half a working week should impinge on his laid-back lifestyle too much.

He was met in reception by a quiet, middle-aged man who showed Jeff directly to a desk, gave him a pile of papers, and briefly demonstrated the correct way to enter data on a computer.

"Let me know if you have a problem".

"Can I get a cuppa?".

"You'll need to bring your own tea".

So that was it - staring at a screen all day, no real thought required, not much social interaction. He began to feel bored by 10.30, and looked longingly out the window to distant hills.

At home Et was concerned about his well-being:

"Are you OK ? Tell me all about it".

"Not much to tell. Data entry. Nobody to talk to. No tea".

"You'll get into it".

"I suppose it'll be worth it for the cash, but my eyes are blurred and I'm very tired".

Ethel gave him a big hug:

"Come on, let's have a bath".

"Now you're talking".

10

Et had gone to work at the hotel, leaving Jeff in the cottage alone to experience some much needed battery re-charging. The red-roofed village was exceptionally quiet for a weekend - grey, damp and very, very peaceful. Some of the houses had smoke rising above them, some did not. It wasn't particularly cold for October, but sometimes people just wanted a fire to reassure themselves that even in the back of beyond the flames of life were burning brightly.

Jeff had been a fan of the I Ching for some time, and felt that there was a great deal of wisdom in it. Et always scoffed in her down to earth way, but nothing could dissuade him from dabbling when she was at work. He had no time for religion or anything like that, something just rang true about this ancient Chinese divination.

"Why are you bothering with that ? We're happy aren't we ?", she would say.

"Of course".

"Well ?".

"I don't question you about your motivation for needlepoint".

"Don't be silly !".

"The two things are very similar - the I Ching can be done using needles, sticks, or even coins, and a computer".

"You're impossible".

Jeff had started out using a stick separation method, but now, mainly out of laziness was using a computer. The first thing was to relax and fix a question in your mind, concentrating on that alone. Then the apparently random act of separation, casting or computation. The result is a hexagram(s) of broken and unbroken lines, which after referring to the I Ching book itself gives instant meaning to the seeker's life !

He would never dare ask a really meaningful question like:

'Will Et and Jeff stay together ?'. Anyway, could any result be taken seriously - not according to Et and 99% of right-thinking, country folk.

The computer said: 'Type in your question'. Jeff tried to think, without thinking. He typed: 'How can I find the right way of life now ?'. After focusing on this question and clicking submit, the computer screen displayed hexagram 2 - The Receptive. The I Ching revealed that the 'superior man' must be led and NOT try to lead - 'following brings sublime success, through the perseverance of a mare'.

For Jeff this was easily interpreted as allowing Et to lead him wherever she wanted, and he couldn't think of a sweeter thing, even if it was a load of bollocks ! He believed there must be something in it though - how else could he be living with her, rich in love, if not money ?

In a few hours she would be back, and any delving into the uncertain future could be put aside, as the reality of their love was still stronger than the harshness of some neighbours, family, or the elements.

"Are you tired luv ?".

"Not really. What have you been up to ? Have you fixed that shelf yet ?".

"I just haven't had a moment".

"You've been pissin' about on that bloody computer again, haven't you ?".

"OK, but I really, really love you !".

Et tried not to smile.

Jeff saw the familiar figure of his dad standing outside the cottage, and after warning his beloved, opened the door.

"Alright son ?".

"Yea, come in".

"Thought I'd see how the two of you are getting on".

Jeff had the uncomfortable feeling that always accompanied

any interaction between them, but luckily Et was there to smooth things over.

"Take a seat. Would you like a mug of tea ?".

"I wouldn't say no".

"I'll make it", insisted Jeff, glad of the chance to disappear for a few minutes.

"Are you two alright here then ?", he asked Et.

"We absolutely love it here".

"And our Jeff's got himself a job I hear".

"Hard to believe isn't it ?".

The lazy son came in with three mugs of tea.

"A bit nippy out there", said dad.

"Cold on the scooter into town this morning".

"Earning some real money at last lad".

"That's right".

The conversation lapsed, the fire crackled and spat, and the beck flowed on towards the small river.

"Better be going then".

"Give my love to mum".

"Bye".

"Bye".

11

Though Jeff's job was only part-time he really missed the freedom to wander round their quiet hamlet and the chalk hills beyond. With the weekend approaching he rang the office saying he'd got a severe cold and was unlikely to be back before next week. With the lie told Jeff was released for a precious few days in the wilderness he loved.

"You'll be getting sacked", Et said disapprovingly.

"It's only a couple of days, I'm sure the council tax payers won't suffer".

"What are you going to do with yourself".

"Maybe go for a walk, it's a lovely day".

Et went to work at the hotel; Jeff started to pack a small rucksack with a few sweets and crisps. There didn't seem to be any need for waterproofs as it was a startlingly bright sky. The summer had been so dry, and now in October there was still little sign of substantial rain.

He followed the usual shady lane by the beck, leading eventually to the empty pasture and steep climb to the Brow. Leaves were already thick on the ground, and floating in the shallow chalk-water away from the village. Jeff stopped, listening to the clear beck over white and yellow stone - a familiar sound he'd grown up with, and it always took him closer to the mystery of nature and life.

Soon he arrived at the Roman road high up on the windy Wold. The view on such a clear day was inspiring, he could see thirty miles in three directions - the busy cares of town dwellers were literally remote. Jeff sat down and thought about Et - they'd not seen eye-to-eye over his sick leave, but he knew that tonight any disagreement would be forgotten and they could resume their mostly happy relationship.

It was a mild day, following on from a hot summer, and Jeff

began to nod-off in the coarse grass by the ancient road. As usual on these treks his mind was filled with dreams of half-forgotten civilisations, and the not so civilised. Now the sounds of water were left behind, replaced by the approaching footfalls of the Roman legionnaire.

A car sped past and brought him back to reality, Jeff got up and continued along the ridge looking across the flat vale. He laughed to himself, thinking of the nonsensical office procedures he'd abandoned (if only temporarily). The only thing that made life bearable there was a friendship developing with a mature lady called Emily. She had a great attitude and healthy disrespect for the so-called Management. There was no chance of him straying from Et as they were too much in love, but Emily had a fantastic pair of breasts for a woman of 46.

"How do you manage to look so good ?".

"For an old maid you mean ?!".

"Not at all".

"Simple - don't eat too much, don't drink too much, take plenty of exercise. Do you know I've got a resting pulse of 50 ?".

"Incredible".

"Feel it", Emily took his hand and placed it over her wrist.

"I can't feel anything", Jeff said nervously.

"A little bit this way, that's it".

"Amazing. The only exercise I get is a bit of walking".

"Nothing wrong with that".

Another car went past, and he felt a bit guilty thinking of this delightful colleague. Jeff decided to cut the ramble short and head back to Beck Cottage.

12

Things went from shaky to a little less shaky in the partnership of landlady and landlord at the Little Angel. A relentless regime of lingerie with carefully positioned holes seemed to be slowly bringing Pete back to some sort of reality. It was not that he could ever let go of the obsession with Jane, but Julie was now, Julie was real, warm, and very giving.

Et and Jeff noticed that the pub atmosphere was much happier now, indeed they'd been spending too much money on ale recently. What with karaoke, Country and Western, disco, and quiz night, they barely had enough time to concentrate on getting Beck Cottage how it should be.

There hadn't been too many fights recently either, at least among the clientele. The gloomy atmosphere that had now evaporated led to a period of tranquillity, rather than smashing glasses and fights in the car park.

"Do you fancy the quiz ?".

"Maybe we should have a quiet night at home", Et replied.

"You don't mean it".

"We're not so well-off that we can afford drinking every night".

"Go on, we're only young once".

"You get the fire banked up then, I don't want to come home to a freezing house".

"No problem. Anything for a pint".

"You'll be putting on weight".

"Not if we keep exercising - together !".

Jeff knew that Et didn't take much persuading into having a few jars, she could drink pints with the best of them, and never put on lard. He wasn't quite so lucky, noticing that some clothes were feeling a little tight - nothing a few long walks wouldn't put right.

"What is the capital of Mongolia ?", Pete gave the first question on the microphone.

"Easy, Ulan Bator", said Jeff smugly.

"How do you know that ?".

"Dad. They had the second communist revolution in 1921".

"Why did Prince Charles choose an old bag, when he had a beautiful young wife ?".

"That's not a proper question", someone shouted.

"Can't you take a joke ? OK. How many times have Nottingham Forest won the European Cup ?".

"Any idea ?", asked Et.

"Not sure".

"We don't want to miss out on that gallon of Waggledick !".

"You're right there - I'll try and see another team's sheet".

"Alright, but don't get caught".

It was very warm in the Little Angel bar with a fire roaring in its sooty hearth. Jeff looked at the landlady in a tight white t-shirt that read 'BIG-UNS', and wondered why Pete couldn't keep his mind on family.

"She's not bad looking".

"You keep your eyes on me mister !".

"I was only saying".

"Well don't".

There was a break in the quiz and everybody rushed to replenish empty glasses. A mostly friendly rivalry was in the air, except for the one or two who took the whole thing too seriously. Last year there had been a terrible fight when a quiz team of gypsies gave the wrong response to a question about the Appleby horse fair.

Et watched Pete and Julie chatting, and was glad to see they were both smiling. Even when the kids poked their heads round the door from the family's private quarters, Pete didn't fly off the handle.

"Do you think we could survive something like that ?".

"Like what ?", asked Jeff.

"The skeleton of a lost love in the cupboard".

"We're not old enough for that, I hope".

"You know what I mean".

"Not really. Anyway, I've told you not to keep asking questions about the survival of us, it's unsettling".

"You're right. ? Did you manage to steal any answers ?".

"One or two", Jeff grinned.

13

Saturday started grey and stormy, it was barely light even at eight o' clock. The TV weather said there was an enormous depression sitting over southern Scotland, bringing misery to the north and west. Jeff had been unable to sleep, so left his beloved to rest for a few more hours.

He watched trees thrashing violently in the garden, and rain lashing against the ill-fitting window. Jeff liked to get up first at the weekend and stuff himself with comfort food - bacon, sausage, egg and tomato in thickly cut white bread, smothered in brown sauce.

It was great not to be bothered by parents - he still wasn't fully used to the joys of independent living. Jeff just laid back on the old couch, as the weather did its worst to the fragile tile roof. Even though he couldn't get enough of Et, these precious moments of solitude were worth more than money.

Maybe later he would quietly climb the stairs and slip into bed beside her. She would wake from a dream to a better reality, where they could show love with the passion of youth. Jeff could never tire of her lovely body as she rose above him, and he cupped and nuzzled those delightful breasts.

The wind had become gale, he saw the TV aerial wobbling madly on the house opposite. It was usual in the village to have power cuts under these circumstances, and sure enough the light started to flicker. He wondered how Et could still be asleep, but went on sipping strong coffee, revelling in the wildness outside.

He cleared out the hearth, which was still warm from the night before, screwed-up some newspaper, and heaped kindling.

Soon the fire was coming to life, occasionally blown back on itself by gusts down the chimney.

"That's nice", said Et yawning.

"The power might go off soon, thought I'd better get some heat in here".

"We don't need to go out today, do we ?".

"No. Let's stay in all day and do very little".

"Any bacon left ?".

"I'll make you a butty".

Jeff's brief time alone was ended, but he didn't mind at all - Et was not some unwanted invader, rather his missing other-half. He was happy to make a sandwich, a drink, or run after her in any way - love bound them in tender tendrils - surprisingly strong.

"I like a storm", she said.

"So do I".

"The beck's up".

"No chance of us flooding".

"This cottage did flood in 1953 - according to mum".

"I didn't know that".

"Good job they've dredged the beck recently".

"Nothing to worry about, come and sit with me".

There was no sign of the weather improving, as Et and Jeff huddled together in the small front room, warmed by the big fire.

"Shame there's no lightning", said Jeff.

"Or thunder".

Then the light went out.

"Shit !".

"Probably be back on soon", reassured Jeff.

"Maybe. Ten o' clock in the morning, and not even light enough to read !".

"It's atmospheric, don't you think ? Branches scraping at the window like the fingernails of an escaped madman".

"You're the bloody madman".

"I'm very well balanced, when you think of all the in-breeding round here".

The light came back on for a moment, but then went off again.

"I'll put another log on", said Jeff.

14

Now TV weather said Sunday was going to be unseasonably warm and bright, so Et borrowed her mum's rusty Austin Maestro for a trip to the coast. She would have preferred to blast up the main road, but Jeff insisted on a bizarre moorland route involving fords and gated roads.

There was nothing he liked more than a thin road with grass growing down the middle, which frequently infuriated Et who was the one forced to negotiate these rough lanes of sheep and tractors.

They took the route by the steam railway out of Pickering, which all being well would eventually arrive at Whitby. On the left Jeff pointed to all the old carriages in various stages of restoration.

"Fascinating", said Et.

"Just relax and enjoy the scenery".

"It's going to take bloody ages to get there".

"Better than the A-road with thousands of weekend tourists".

As they drove further and further out towards the moors, scenery began to become more wild and unforgiving. It wasn't long before they reached the edge of the forest, and the first ford that didn't have more than a few inches of water running over the road bed.

"Disappointing water levels", Jeff remarked.

"Not for this car, it can't cope with anything deeper".

They pulled-up at the first gate, and Jeff jumped out to remove the chain. It was late morning, and warm October sunshine filled his heart with joy.

"Isn't this better than the main drag ?".

"Maybe".

Now they were up on the barren moors with fantastic views in all directions.

"Watch that sheep !", Jeff screamed.

"Calm down, I wasn't anywhere near it".

It wasn't long before they approached a deeper ford, at the bottom of a steep valley.

"Not sure about this one".

"Just drive very fast", said Jeff.

"Are you mad ? It's not you behind the wheel".

"Go on !".

In truth the water was only about six inches deep, but to a rusty heap it might pose a serious challenge.

"There we go, no problem".

As Jeff finished speaking the car started to cough and came to an abrupt halt.

"Now what ?".

"Let's pull over and have some sarnies".

"What do you mean pull over ? We've bloody stopped !".

"Good job there's no traffic. I'm sure it'll be fine after a rest".

So they stayed in the car, in the middle of an otherwise empty road and opened the packed lunch.

"Wonderful".

"What is ?", Et asked abruptly.

"Out here in the middle of nowhere".

"Good job you like it, we could be here for a while".

"I've got the mobile, we can ring the AA".

"You won't get a bloody signal here !", she snapped.

The car went quiet for a while, as they munched cheese sandwiches, and sheep munched grass outside, bleating occasionally.

"We're going to be stuck here all night".

"Someone will come past".

"Have you seen anybody since we left Pickering ?".

"Not exactly".

"We'll be hungry and cold".

"I think there are some mints in the glove compartment, and a rug in the boot".

"It must be at least twenty miles to the nearest village", Et worried.

"I'd say more like nineteen".

"That's reassuring".

The afternoon was now quite warm, Jeff wandered back to the stream alone. He stood in the middle of the little footbridge, looking down into the chill, clear water. Engines were not really his thing, so there seemed no point looking under the bonnet and giving Et false hope.

He heard her try to start the Maestro a couple of times, then silence except for sheep or the occasional manic flapping of a startled grouse. Then the engine sprang into life.

"Quick !", shouted Et, and he dashed back to the car.

"How did you manage that ?".

"Never mind, just get in, we might make Whitby by dark".

The temperamental vehicle began to pull away from the valley bottom, and was soon speeding along the ridge at 30mph. In the distance they could see Abbey ruins on the cliff top.

"Doesn't look far now".

"Maybe fifteen miles", replied Jeff.

"We're coming back on the main road".

"If you insist".

15

It was getting dark as they parked in a side street on the West Cliff at Whitby. Normally they would go nearer the railway station, but Jeff had heard something about an Art Deco cafe in this part of town.

"It's bloody freezing !", Et shivered.

"Look at the size of those waves !", said Jeff, pointing towards the harbour mouth.

They had a fantastic view through the whale bone arch across murky water to the ruined Abbey and church. More and more lights were coming on, rippling down into icy depths.

"Shall we stay over ?".

"Can we afford it ?", Et replied.

"Dave mentioned a cheap place not far away - great views across the water".

"It'll be good not to drive back in the dark. Are you sure this B&B is alright ? Is it for bikers ?".

"Just because Dave stayed there, don't assume it'll be all helmets and leathers - he does have a softer side".

"He does ?!".

They wandered around narrow streets, but there was no sign of the cafe. It was now completely dark and the wind slashed their cheeks and foreheads. It was hard to imagine how fishermen could earn a living on these harsh seas, and those much harsher.

"Can we check-in at the hotel and get something to eat ?".

"Sure", Jeff replied cheerfully.

"What's the place called ?".

"The Alucard".

"Peculiar name".

"It is".

They came to a crescent of houses that were tall and poorly lit, in the middle was the crumbling three-storey Alucard. Jeff led the way up a flight of ten steps to a massive black front door.

"Do you think this is a good idea ? We could still drive back".

"Don't be a baby. I'll buy you a Lucky Duck tomorrow".

"How can I resist such a generous offer !", said Et.

The door was opened by a small, smiling old lady who stank of stale urine. They looked beyond her into a cavernous hall lit by only one candle. Both wished they'd gone back to the car, but it was too late.

She led them very slowly to the first floor; despite the smell Et and Jeff took to the old woman immediately, after all she wasn't to blame for being past it.

"Only got two singles", she said quietly.

"Fine", said Et.

"Fine", muttered Jeff, thinking he might miss out on a shag.

"I'll leave you to it then - it's number 8 and number 8b. We don't bother to lock the front door, so if you're off to the pub no need to worry".

"Thanks", both replied.

Et and Jeff went into number 8.

"We might as well share".

"I knew you'd say that", Et said.

"Rather basic, and a bit smelly".

"It'll do for one night. I'll just go to the toilet and we can go out for a drink".

Jeff was left alone in near darkness, listening to icy wind tugging at the shutters. Everything seemed to be covered in dust, even the bed covers that hadn't been changed for God knows how long. There was a loud bang from downstairs and he jumped up.

"What the fuck ?!".

"What was that ?", asked Et coming back to the room.

"I don't know, but let's go to the pub".

They walked into town away from cliffs and wild sea battering the harbour wall. In the shelter of back streets it felt a little warmer, as smoke from kipper sheds filled the air. Some of the shops seemed to be about fifty years behind those found at designer outlets - windows covered in amber cellophane.

"Bloody hell !", Jeff shouted.

"What ?".

"The Little Angel".

"It's not our Little Angel".

Et refused to go in on the grounds that it wouldn't be as good as their local. She made him walk further down towards the River Esk and swivel bridge leading to the Abbey side.

"Do you know where we're going ?".

"Not really".

"I'm hungry, let's get some fish and chips".

As it was much cheaper to buy them from a chippy rather than go for a sit-down meal, Jeff bought fish and chips twice with a mountain of scraps on each. They wandered round near-deserted streets, trying desperately to keep out of the biting wind.

Finally, they made it into a tiny pub on a cobbled road leading towards the famed 199 steps. Jeff was relieved that the bar jammed with locals didn't fall silent as they entered, instead they were greeted warmly by the plump landlady.

"Two pints please".

"Bit cold out there luvs", she said.

"Yes", Et smiled back.

"You can have a nice warm by the fire. Are you staying in town ?".

"The Alucard", Jeff replied.

The vibrant bar didn't exactly hush at this revelation, but both of them sensed ears being pricked. Et pushed her way into the snug, followed by Jeff and the beers.

"Did you notice the reaction ?".

"Very strange", admitted Jeff.

They didn't really know what to make of it, and so sat back in front of a lovely log fire, supping quietly.

"I'd like to live in Whitby".

"Too many tourists in the summer", Jeff replied.

"Not near those massive houses up by the park".

"How could we afford that ?".

"A large-scale prostitution racket. We could ship teenagers in from the Baltic states".

"That's mad".

"Not at all. It'd be like 21st century whaling, without the whales".

"Maybe environmentally friendly, but I'm not too keen on harpooning youngsters for the sex trade".

"OK. You stay in that crummy office, and I'll carry on at the hotel".

Jeff enjoyed the verbal fencing they sometimes indulged in, but even for him prostitution didn't seem quite right.

"I'll get some more beers".

"You do that", Et snapped.

He went from the empty, warm snug into the loud, heaving bar.

"Same again luv ?".

"Thanks".

"I'm surprised you're staying at that Alucard, funny goings on up there !".

"What do you mean ?".

"Well, you've only got to look at the name".

"What's wrong with it ?".

"Try spelling it the other way".

Jeff took the pints and went back to the snug.

"Alucard backwards.............it spells Dracula !".

"I thought you knew that already".

"You've known all along ?".

"It's only a story, what are you afraid of ?".

"Nothing, but the place does seem a bit weird".

"Don't worry you can cuddle up to me. Unless you'd rather sleep in 8b on your own ?".

"No, I'll stick with you".

Back at the Alucard and the relative safety of their room, Jeff and Et were overcome by uncontrollable giggling, brought on by a mixture of local ale and the relief at not having their necks bitten - at least not yet.

"You're drunk", Jeff observed.

"You're pissed".

"You're sozzled".

"You're intoxicwated", Et almost said.

Though the room wasn't warm, at least the smell of urine had gone to bed hours ago. Jeff was surprised to find the electric light worked, and wondered why the old woman had been burning a candle earlier. Et looked particularly alluring in her white bra and panties, but he wasn't sure if it was possible to get undressed by himself after the powerful ale.

"Help me !".

"You're pathetic, I don't want you inside me tonight".

"Please, help me !".

They both burst out laughing again, and Jeff tripped over while removing his jeans.

16

They had both enjoyed a great trip to the coast, and wished it was a full week rather than one night in a run-down, questionably evil establishment. No wonder Whitby was crawling with tourists during the day at virtually any time of year, it had so many of the ingredients that result in the perfect British seaside resort - and a few peculiar ones thrown in too.

Et and Jeff were so happy; yet he still took the opportunity of his first time alone at home to reach for the trusty I Ching. He didn't know himself why this happiness couldn't be just enjoyed, and perpetual delving into the future ditched.

It was good to be back at their cottage though, despite the fact that the return brought with it a large helping of reality. At least Jeff could sit at the computer and look out over their tiny beck, drifting off into the mystery that lay somewhere in his beloved hills.

'How can I be happy now ?' he typed into the I Ching box - a question which would easily be answered when Et came back from the hotel. Nonetheless, he persisted in the folly, masquerading as enlightenment.

Jeff clicked the button, submitting his question to the unknown, but nothing happened, the PC froze - he had his answer in the form of a technological refusal. Maybe an unseen hand *was* trying to tell him something, or was it simply that his hard disk needed defragmenting.

The computer wasn't exactly new, a special offer from Gigantic Technology in Pocklington eleven miles along the chalk ridge. Often he would switch on and get one of a hundred different error messages - eventually having to flick a switch on the wall and start again - the joy of modern electricals !

"Sod it !", he shouted to the empty house.

Rather than trying again Jeff decided to take a walk along the ridge near Hanging Grimston and its gated roads. Up there he could forget about the modern world, or at least keep it in distant view over the flat vale spreading out below.

As always it was a tough climb up from the village, and the cloudy early winter's day did not give spectacular views - but these modest ones were enough to enrich the soul. Jeff realised he would have to go into the office tomorrow, and wasn't relishing the prospect of an icy scooter ride in the dark, followed by mind-numbing data processing.

Some people claimed to be good at leaving worries behind, but he always found it difficult to live in the moment, like a tiger hunting its prey. Usually though, as these walks progressed the rhythm of nature was kind to him, and gradually concerns would slip away as he focussed on a kestrel hovering over the verge, or a big brown hare sprint across a field.

"Can you tell me the way to the animal artist ?". A car had pulled-up with two old folk in.

"Just follow the signs", Jeff replied cheerily.

"We haven't seen any", the silver-haired driver replied.

He was immediately concerned about the eyesight of these pensioners, as whenever this local artist held a sale of work he would plaster the countryside with direction boards. If they couldn't see them, surely they were not safe to drive !

"Take the next road on the right and drive for about 3 miles, then left for another mile".

"Thank you young man".

Jeff smiled to himself as the old couple ignored his advice, setting off in completely the wrong direction.

"Deaf as well as blind", he muttered to himself.

Et had always said what a lucky bastard this guy was, spending all his time painting animals, and earning a decent living too - with the help of a few Government grants. Shame that neither of them had any aptitudes that might allow an independent life.

It started to drizzle, but Jeff wasn't bothered as he'd come out in some decent clothing that could cope with most weather. He decided to drop down off the Wold top, opening the gate that led into green sheep pasture below Hanging Grimston. He suspected that the rather gruesome name was nothing to do with capital punishment, more the way this place appeared to hang in the air or suspend itself from the high Wold.

He'd often wondered what it would be like living in the remote farmhouse below - perhaps too lonely during the unforgiving winter months. It would be good to be the only habitation in your own valley though, but the nearest pub was five miles away - maybe not such a good idea after all.

It seemed a long time since he'd visited the springs at Millington with Et; now the landscape was bleak, even though the small hills still managed to be beautiful in the windswept chill of November. As he remembered their summer splashing, Jeff began to yearn for Beck Cottage again, and wished the hours away till she got back from hotel scivvying.

He now felt torn between the call of dismal, raw nature, and the warm hearth of their modest home.

"I'll just loop through Kirby Underdale", he said to himself. "Maybe the post office will be open".

Jeff liked the way this tiny hamlet clung to its little hillocks, with the ancient church a splendid centrepiece. It was far smaller than their own village, but at least it had a shop where the weary rambler could get a drink and something to eat.

The afternoon was chilly, but he enjoyed sitting by the road supping from a can and munching a chocolate bar. A lone farmer waved as he noisily passed by on a tractor, but there was nobody else for miles. It would take about two hours to get back through Deepdale, just before dark, just before Et came home.

17

When Et and Jeff got to the Little Angel that night at 9.15 they were astonished to see the pub in darkness. Et had a look through the bar window.

"I can see somebody in there".

"What are they doing in the dark ?".

"Just sitting", Et replied.

Jeff pushed opened the heavy front door slowly, not sure what was going on.

"Hello".

"Go away !", a female voice shouted. It was Julie, the landlady.

Et pushed him in, and quickly followed behind.

"It's Jeff and Et, no need to worry. What's wrong ?".

"Nothing a few more bottles of this won't solve".

Even though the bar was unlit, Julie was a pitiful sight swigging from a bottle of gin.

"Where's Pete ?", asked Jeff.

"I don't know where that bastard is, and I don't care !".

"You don't mean that", Et said, putting her arm round the sobbing landlady.

"I fuckin' do ! He's fucked off with that fuckin' tart he used to know".

"Are you sure ?", Et asked.

"Course I'm fucking sure, what do you think he's been dreaming of doing this last year ?".

While Et was consoling Julie, Jeff nipped behind the bar and poured two large whiskies to soothe their own sense of shock. They'd both thought the couple were putting Pete's fantasy behind them, and the pub was getting back to normal.

"Anybody there ?".

"That's all we need, those two puffs", Jeff snarled.

"Anything wrong ?", Roger asked.

"You two had better come into the back with me".

"That's an offer we can't refuse", said Paul.

Jeff led them into the lounge, leaving Et to get the whole painful story, and try to help Julie with her devastation. Roger and Paul were now looking more serious.

"Pete's buggered off then ?", said Roger.

"Funny way of putting it", Paul chipped in.

"Leave it Paul, this is not a time for jokes". Roger looked a little angry, regarding the landlord and landlady as friends.

"I don't really know anything, Et is just finding out..........I know he was crazy about this Jane".

"Where are the kids ?", asked Roger.

"No idea", Jeff replied.

Roger went upstairs to see everything was OK, and was delighted to find the young ones fast asleep.

"He must be mad, running off like that", said Paul, filling the silence.

Jeff didn't reply, he wasn't inclined to speculate about Pete - they had become quite close following all their chats about the past - he couldn't believe it had come to this.

Et came into the lounge, leaving Julie with her gin.

"She's in a bad way, I think we'll have to call her sister".

"Good idea", said Roger coming down stairs.

"I'll stay with her, I can give the hotel a miss tomorrow", Et volunteered.

Jeff gave her a peck on the cheek, and the three men slipped out the side door.

"He must be mad", Paul repeated in the dark main street.

"Maybe", said Roger sadly.

"He loves Jane, that's the problem", Jeff said firmly.

18

Et came back home at just after 9 o'clock in the morning looking absolutely worn out, with puffy, red eyes, as though she had been doing all the crying.

"You look awful".

"Thanks alot".

"How is she ?".

"Well, at least her sister's there now".

"I'll make you a cuppa".

"Bastard !".

"What ?!".

"Not you - him !".

"He really loves this other woman".

"And that justifies leaving kids, and a wife in that state ?".

Jeff let the question hang in the air, because he knew that it couldn't be right either way.

"I'll get that tea".

Et slumped in a chair, too exhausted and disappointed to know anything with certainty. It was hard for her to understand how this sort of thing could happen, as she was so happy with Jeff - she had so little experience of what others called the 'real world'.

She also knew that Jeff was even worse - as far removed from reality as it's possible to be without being committed to an asylum by two doctors who know what's best.

"Drink this, you'll feel better. I've put some bacon on".

"I'm not hungry", she said wearily.

"It's that nice bacon from Mount Pleasant Farm".

"Whatever".

Jeff sat on the chair arm and tried to comfort her, but his beloved was really fed up. A gentle knock at the door distracted them, he got up to find his mother standing there.

"What is it ?".

"It's your father, he's.......er, he's been arrested".

"Jesus Christ ! What's he done now ?".

Et guided her to a chair, and poured a large glass of cheap brandy.

"It's those camera mobile phones. He was caught holding one upside-down with the screen angled to look up a woman's skirt".

"That's terrible", said Et.

"I'm so ashamed".

"Don't blame yourself mum".

Jeff couldn't immediately identify a problem in what he'd heard, but supposed some people might be a bit sensitive about having their knickers snapped, and potentially sent over the mobile airwaves to a perverted recipient.

"He was the same on holiday in Cornwall in 1967".

"But these phones have only just come out", said Et.

"It was all done with mirrors and a cheap Kodak in those days. I begged him to get professional help".

"You mean David Bailey or Lord Lichfield ?".

"Shut up Jeff, you're not helping", snapped Et.

"It's alright, have some brandy", she tried to comfort his sobbing mother.

Et couldn't believe she was having to console another innocent victim of male sexuality gone haywire.

"Have they released him yet ?", asked Jeff.

"No, they've taken him to the Police station on Fulford Rd.. They've put him in one of those white paper boiler suits".

"Fascists !", spat Jeff.

"Try some more", Et kept giving her more spirit in the hope of some magical cure to the predicament.

"You can stay here for now, we'll ring the Police this afternoon", suggested Jeff.

"Thanks luv, I don't want to be a bother".

The three of them sat quietly in front of a low-burning coal fire - Et too emotionally drained, mother numbed, and Jeff afraid of saying something light-hearted. After ten minutes Et made excuses and went for a lie down.

"I don't know why you stay with him".

"A bad habit, like smoking".

"Seriously though, why bother ?".

"We've been together thirty years, I can't just give up".

"Well I bloody have".

"Don't say that son. He's not all bad".

Jeff thought about his childhood spoiled by the behaviour of this man who'd become a stranger. If he wasn't beating mother, he was beating him, and for no good reason other than his failure to achieve anything in life except an unhappy family.

"He doesn't even like mobile phones, he's always complaining about people using them in public".

"It wasn't really the phone he was interested in".

"Stupid old sod".

"There's no need for you to get upset; he'll have to take what's coming to him".

"If he does go to prison at least it'll be a break for you".

She didn't reply, just looked into the small flames, occasionally trying to sip from an empty glass.

19

Jeff's dad was eventually released by the Police, with the prospect of a trial some months ahead. Et persuaded his mum to stay on with them, even though it was a tight squeeze in the small cottage.

She would have gone straight back to him if it hadn't been for the interference of the young 'uns; brought up in the days where a wife stood by her husband (even if he did try to take pictures of pants outside the immediate family).

Jeff was glad to escape it all by scootering off to the office, while Et added to her 'sick' time from the hotel. He hadn't expected that work could sometimes be an escape from problems at home - the mother he loved, but wouldn't let him breathe - the father he hated more and more.

Tacky Christmas decorations were already on display round their cramped workstations, and female colleagues seemed to take longer and longer lunch breaks to buy presents. Emily did not fall in with the rest, preferring to take a more laid-back route to Yuletide joy. Jeff could still not believe how wonderful she looked, being nearly the same age as his mum. He knew it was essential to avoid the mistletoe in the tea room, or it might prove impossible not to succumb to her mature charms !

"Are you having Christmas dinner with your parents ?", Emily asked.

"Probably just the two of us; mum will be back with him by then. What about you ?".

"Just a quiet time alone with the Queen's speech".

"You've got loads of contacts".

"Contacts maybe, but nobody special".

Jeff couldn't help gazing at her full breasts in a rather obvious manner, following the cleavage down as far as possible without shoving his nose in there.

"You're a lucky boy Jeffrey".

"Yes, I know".

"Don't end up lonely like me".

"How could you be lonely ? I mean.......somebody like you".

He looked into dark eyes, and quickly away again, frightened of falling too far into her mysterious soul.

Jeff found another escape in the tedious data that never stopped flowing in from their vast rural area. He tried to focus on only this, letting thoughts of Et, family and a sensuous co-worker slip away like a half-finished boat from a forgotten shipyard.

A few more days of mind-numbing figures, and he'd be ready for a two-week break of excessive food and drink, sprinkled with an argument or two. Emily could continue with her lonely, siren song, but he was and would remain a one woman man - unless there was too much free booze at the office party......

"How's mum been ?".

"I think she's more than ready to go home", said Et.

"You're right, but I can't bear to think about him".

"He is your dad".

"Well, I'm not buying him any after-shave this year".

"It won't spoil our first Christmas !".

"Just the two of us".

"What do you fancy, Turkey or Duck ?".

"Not enough meat on a duck. Anyway, I don't care as long as we can spend some special time together !".

"What do you mean ?!".

"Playing Monopoly - something like that".

20

The Sunday before Christmas started with blue sky, but the radio promised snow for the afternoon. The wind was getting-up, with shrunken garden plants tossing ever more violently. It was eleven o' clock, but not even a dog walker ventured out, as if villagers knew it was time to light fires and batten down the hatches.

"If we get a good fall, neither of us will have to go to work next week".

"Ever the optimist", said Et.

"I can't face even the two days".

"Part-timer !".

"I was happier before, just left to wander about".

"How sad ! But we do need the cash for food and so on".

Jeff always found himself stunned by the blunt weapon of reality, but he never let go of the precious inner world that made him unique. Without a dreamworld how could he go on ? Jeff would never accept that there was no more to life than work and a pension.

The beck had been replenished by heavy rain, and he didn't care about the threats of drought next summer. Jeff liked to watch the water rushing by, gazing at the chalky bottom for a glint of metal that might take him back to another time, before cars and giant supermarkets.

"You've gone quiet".

"Just thinking".

"About me ?".

"No".

"That's nice".

She kissed him, and moved Jeff's right hand onto her left breast.

"What are you doing ?".

"Santa's come early".

"Premature ejaculation !?".

"Don't be silly. Let's go back to bed".

"It is turning colder".

The afternoon was grey and bitter, snow was already reported on the Moors and coast, and Jeff waited at the window for the first flakes. He watched vast clouds moving quickly south west, but underneath it all the village still seemed empty.

"We need some more coal", Et shouted.

His forehead was a poor match for savage wind, and he wished that the hat Et had bought wasn't lost in the cottage as usual. In the distance Jeff heard wind chimes frantically trying to keep in tune with the elements. He looked up at the sky, but no snow came to transform the familiar scene.

"Don't go out there !".

"I wasn't planning to", Et replied.

"No sign of snow".

"Maybe overnight".

"Have you bought me anything nice ?".

"You're so impatient. Can't you wait just a few more days ?".

"No".

"Well, don't go looking in the cupboards".

Et looked out and saw a youngish lady delivering cards with a toddler running behind, carrying a little pink bag.

"Who's that ?".

"No idea", said Jeff without bothering to get up.

The little boy fell over and started to cry, and mummy picked him up.

"Would you like children ?".

"Not yet, we're too young".

"I would".

"We can't afford it. Anyway, I want your body all to myself".

"You'd make a good dad".

"Do you think so ?".

Jeff was more interested in a heavy snowfall and missing the last days of work before Christmas Day. Et was busy planning a family of two girls and two boys.

'Just a couple of inches can bring immense pleasure', as the village ex-nun remarked every festive season. Et insisted that this comment referred to snow and the joy children could experience, coupled with the visual transformation for all.

When Jeff looked out of the curtains the following morning at just before six, there had been a light snowfall, as yet untouched by human foot or car wheels. It wouldn't be properly light for two hours, but missing work was certain.

"It's snowed Et".

She was fast asleep.

"Maybe an inch".

She didn't stir. Jeff went to the kitchen to make coffee; and then sat in the lounge absorbing the extraordinary silence under their snowy Wold.

21

After breakfast they got the long wooden sledge (bought from a boat yard in Norfolk) out of summer storage, and started up Beck Lane towards the Wold foot. It was a grey morning, but they didn't really expect any further snow as the TV weather said all would turn to rain by evening. Et and Jeff were well togged-up in wellies and long, thick coats, ready for a couple of hours near the Wold top.

"I'm not used to exercise !", puffed Jeff.

"No, you don't do much".

"I don't have chance to use the hotel swimming pool like you".

"You can't swim".

They could see a few kids hundreds of feet above them, turning the soft, thin covering of snow into a sheet of polished ice. Young voices rang round the little hills like high-pitched bells from Burythorpe church in the distance.

"Slow down Jeff".

"I thought you were the fit one ?".

They stopped, and looked back over the tiny village, and further into the white blur that eventually became a town. Et gave him a squeeze round the waist.

"I love you".

"I love you".

How could anyone not love her young, uncomplicated face ? With red cheeks and nose, courtesy of an icy blast direct from Lapland. They hugged in the wilderness of middle Wold, while everything seemed to be dead around them, except for those shouts drifting down from the high slopes.

Et started to run, but after a few yards fell over into deeper snow away from the path they could hardly follow. Jeff went after her, diving down, grabbing, and rolling over and over in uncontrollable laughter.

"Stop it ! We'll get cold".

"I don't care", he shouted.

Jeff kissed her on the lips, and then took-off with the sledge to join the kids.

"Hang on, I'm coming".

"Hurry up".

The last part of the climb was the worst - much steeper and more difficult to stay on your feet. They knew all the kids pretty well as the village was a tight-knit community, though that didn't stop them being cheeky little bastards. A couple of the older ones were aiming their sledges directly at Et and Jeff, trying to knock them over.

"I'll do for that sod !".

"They're just having fun", said Et laughing.

"Did we behave like that at eleven ?".

"You probably did".

They finally reached the thin, flattish 'launch pad' at the top, and Et climbed on the front, wedging her wellies onto the front runners. Jeff got on carefully behind, holding tight round her belly and fixing his own feet in the middle.

"Are you ready ?".

"Not really", Et replied nervously.

Jeff gave one big push with his right leg - immediately they began to gather speed on the short, steep section. The problem was going to be negotiating the small dip, followed by a long, shallower descent.

"Are you OK ?".

Et could only scream as they cleared the ground by a couple of inches, then landed safely on the flatter surface. Jeff leaned to the right, trying to steer the sledge towards the valley bottom - suddenly they were in a heap and laughing loudly.

"Fantastic", said Jeff.

"Not bad. It's your fault we came off though".

"It won't take long to get back up".

"I'm knackered already !".

It started to rain, and then heavily, the kids soon dashed back towards the village, slipping and sliding as they went. Et and Jeff were not far behind, sledging part of the way and then walking as they came towards Beck Lane.

Jeff was exhilarated by their little, clear stream that had grown into a winter torrent, fed by all the run-off from the Wold. A bubbling cauldron of water had gathered above the village, swirling in a rough chalk bowl, before racing towards the swelling river miles below.

They were both thoroughly soaked, and now muddy, as the snow started to melt under torrential rain.

"We can get the fire going, and make a pot of tea".

"I'm going to tear-off your clothes !", shouted Jeff.

"You'll have a job, they're welded to me".

22

On Christmas Eve Et had been summoned to work at the hotel, and she dared not disappoint the sour management. Jeff should have gone to work, but phoned in with a stomach bug.

"You'll be getting sacked", she warned him.

"It'll be fine".

As soon as Et had left home, he started to get ready for one of the walks that didn't seem to happen very often these days. He rode his motorbike up the steep hill out of the village, then down through Birdsall estate, and east towards Wharram. The morning was grey and mild, and it was a pleasant trip to the old Malton-Driffield railway line.

Jeff's intention was to walk to the deserted medieval settlement of Wharram Percy, approaching via the dismantled railway rather than the main 'tourist' entrance. Even though this famous historical site was only a couple of miles from home, he'd only visited once before.

Nobody was about, not even a man and dog, as he walked the flat track bed, past the huge, derelict, concrete chalk silos. Jeff could quite easily picture steam trains through the valley, as it was only a few decades since the last non-passenger services. It was more difficult to envisage life in the abandoned village beyond, that had ceased centuries ago.

After an hour's easy walking he came to the wooden gate that led up a short incline to Wharram Percy itself. He was a little nervous because of cattle grazing near the broad, grassy path, and tried to determine if they were docile cows, or cows and a raging bull.

Walking slowly, Jeff managed to avoid any attack from the animals that were really only interested in grass. He came to the first explanatory notice showing a significant settlement up and to the right, with a 'modern' stone cottage immediately in front (that had the Wharram railway sign on), and ruined church with fish pond and stream beyond that.

He poked his nose in the empty, roofless church, which felt like a good setting for a vampire movie. Jeff continued through a few gravestones, and finally found a seat in front of the large pond. He took out some cheese sandwiches and a flask of tea, feeling a little tired, but also privileged to be alone in this unique environment.

There didn't appear to be an explanation on the information boards as to why the village had been deserted. Jeff thought it was too far to the nearest shop or takeaway; it made their village look like a city ! If the medieval population could only have been patient - in the late 1800's a railway would arrive providing convenient access to Driffield or Malton. Thinking more seriously, Jeff thought disease must have been the primary reason for abandoning the tiny hamlet sheltered from the high Wolds.

It felt strange to be in this wilderness on Christmas Eve, while Et toiled at the hotel, waiting on the chubby, cheerful guests. He watched a heron fishing the shallows, and dare not move from the hard, wooden seat.

The bird disappeared towards Thixendale, and Jeff packed his rucksack to walk back. As he stood, a kind of dizziness blurred his vision for a moment, and was sure that for a second he glimpsed on the ridge some ragged ancestors working the difficult, chalky soil. At first Jeff was scared, feeling vulnerable and remote from Et, but soon he truly felt part of the hills, trees, water and people - then and now.

23

It was dark by the time he got back to Beck Cottage, and the evening was turning icy. Because there was no street lighting the clear sky seemed to be brimming with stars. Jeff knew Et must be home as the front window flickered light from the open fire.

"You're late".

"I've been over to Wharram".

"Can't you do something normal, like go shopping ?".

"You wouldn't want me to be normal".

Et had made a lovely job of the decorations, particularly a little tree next to the fire, that he'd nicked from the plantation - well, they wouldn't miss one or two. She was keen to make their first Christmas special, even if they didn't have much cash to throw around.

"What do you think ?".

"Beautiful........like you".

"You're taking the piss !".

"No, I love you".

She knew he meant it; and that their short time in the cottage had been mostly bliss - not wedded bliss, not yet - just the joy of two young people coming to appreciate each other.

"I'll make a pot of tea", said Jeff.

"There are some fruit scones in the cupboard".

Even though they would be alone for Christmas dinner, the small kitchen was bursting with food and drink, including an enormous turkey they'd got from the farm over Leppington way. Jeff could hardly close the fridge door after using the milk, and there was no space to cut and butter scones.

"Are you sure you haven't invited anyone else ?", he shouted.

"You're a greedy sod, I'm sure it'll soon disappear".

He returned to the fire with a tray, and sat close to Et.

"So what were you doing at Wharram ?".

"Just a walk. There was no bugger else there".

"That's a surprise on Christmas Eve".

He decided not to mention the light-headed moment, when it appeared past and present had collided in the remote valley. It wasn't the time for a 'debate' with Et, who had no patience with the supernatural. Neither of them were at all religious, so they were no different to the millions of others getting ready for the Christmas feast.

"I haven't been up there for years. I remember loads of archaeologists scraping the mud with trowels, when we went with school".

"If it snows again over Christmas, we could both go and sample the strange atmosphere", suggested Jeff.

"We'd never be able to get there on those back roads, even with a slight fall. What do you mean by strange atmosphere anyway ?".

"Nothing really. It's just so cut-off from anywhere".

"Exactly".

When Jeff came back from the loo Et had put the TV on, which as far as he was concerned ruined the possibility of anything magical happening. How could the silly plot of Emmerdale, with its petty intrigues of Yorkshire farming folk not kill the festive mood ?

"If Dennis Norden's fuckin' Laughter File comes on I'm going out !".

"That's not till after Boxing Day".

A knock at the door saved Jeff from death by television - his mate Dave was grinning at the door.

"What are you so cheery about ?".

"Just my happy nature", Dave replied.

"Get yourself in then".

Jeff brought three beers from the kitchen.

"Did you know that the Little Angel's open again ?".

"Has Pete come back ?!", asked Et.

"Not sure, but the pub's definitely open tonight".

"Great, let's all go", said Jeff.

"Fine with me", Et smiled.

Et in particular was dying to know if they'd got back together, or maybe Julie had decided to simply get on with her life and run the place with more hired help.

It was nine o' clock by the time the three of them made it up there, and it sounded pretty lively even from outside. Dave pushed open the door, and they all fought their way through a crowd to the bar.

"I'll get the first round", insisted Dave.

Et spotted Julie sitting near the fire, and wasted no time in going straight over to find out the full story.

"Hi luv", said Julie warmly.

"Has he come back then ?".

"Not a bloody card - nothin' ".

"You decided to open up though".

"Well, you can't let men ruin your life".

"What about the kids ?".

"Asleep upstairs, they're fine".

Dave and Jeff came through to join them.

"Alright lads ?".

"Very well", said Dave for both of them.

"You're doing a good trade tonight", Jeff observed.

"Yea, and we won't be stopping at eleven !".

All the punters seemed to be in good heart, and with Christmas Day only a few hours off there was a fair chance of no trouble. Slade came on the juke box again with their festive hit, and virtually the whole pub joined in.

Jeff was well on the way to getting pissed, when Et said she wanted to be in bed asleep by midnight.

"But it's just getting going", he pleaded.

"You can stay if you like".

"No, I'm coming - I'll just say goodbye to Dave".

They went out the side door virtually unnoticed, and Jeff looked up at the countless stars, while Et tied a boot lace.

"You're frightened of missing Father Christmas !".

"It's not that.......".

"What then ?".

"I don't know, it just feels wrong to be partying into Christmas Day - it's not New Year's Eve".

With a slip here and a slide there, they made it back to the warm cottage and low burning fire. Jeff chucked some coal on, and they went straight upstairs into a world where dreams came easily.

24

"Turkey's off ".

"What do you mean ?", said Et, just waking.

"The bloody power's off !".

"Shit".

"I've had the battery radio on - they say about 4,000 homes are affected round here".

"When will it be back on ?".

"They can't say".

Et felt sad that their first Christmas Day together would be ruined by some moderate winds the night before.

"What are the power lines made of ?".

"Clearly nothing substantial", Jeff replied.

"It'll have to be a tin of beans on the camping gas stove".

"Maybe it'll come on soon".

Jeff went to get her present from the cupboard - a micro-CD system in a box big enough for an elephant.

"This'll cheer you up. Apart from the fact you can't plug it in of course !".

Et smiled and tore at the wrapping ferociously.

"That's brilliant, just what I wanted".

"Well, you have dropped one or two hints".

Et reached under the bed for the slim parcel she'd hidden last night.

"Don't know what you'll make of this".

Jeff was pleased to see it wasn't a jumper or underpants, but a DVD player.

"Excellent, about time we moved on from VHS; all we need now is some electricity !".

"Come here and give us a kiss".

"Might as well, not much else to do without power".

It was 9am on a grey, mildish Christmas morning. Virtually

everyone in the village had their fire lit and radio on, desperately hoping for a chance to get a big bird in the oven.

For some reason these power cuts were fairly regular, even though the village was only six miles from the small town and fifteen miles from the big town. If England faced the same weather as Finland there would never be any electricity from our feeble network. It's very rare to get genuinely severe weather in the Yorkshire Wolds, but all that's needed for a cut is a few snow flakes, a little ice, a breath of wind.

"We can have the bird tomorrow".

"Or the next day".

"The power won't be off that long will it ?".

"They simply cannot say", said Jeff.

"How many candles have we got ?".

"Your mum gave us five boxes".

"What about booze ?".

"Plenty".

"Coal, logs ?".

"Stop worrying ! This is NOT a life or death situation".

"I just wanted it to be special".

"It will be".

Jeff went down to stoke the fire, smiling to himself at the magic of their 'predicament'. So what if the power was off for a few days - it would be hard for older or poorly folk - but Et and Jeff had each other, a good fire, plenty of food and drink. Instead of the focus being endless television, they would have to explore other ways to amuse themselves.

25

When Jeff got up at around 3am on Boxing Day to go for a pee, the bathroom light suddenly came on and gave him a shock.

"It's back then", Et said, as he climbed into bed.

"Yea, I was getting a bit fed-up of candles".

Et was up at first light before eight to switch the oven on, determined they would have a proper Christmas dinner one day late. Outside it looked like another grey morning - she gave the fire a few pokes and chucked a log on.

"Everything OK ?".

"Fine. I'll pop the bird in soon".

Jeff pressed his swollen cock gently against her behind.

"What's that ?!".

"A late present".

"For you maybe".

She laughed and turned her body towards him, looking deeply into familiar eyes for a connection. Jeff kissed her in a way that felt unique even though the act had been repeated so many times, and she responded with wild tenderness.

After a short sleep she went to the kitchen and loaded their large lunch into the oven. Et calculated that the meal would be ready about 2pm, allowing them to finish by three for the Queen's speech. It seemed the elderly monarch was obliged by advisers to become more and more 'hip' each year. Et wondered if this time she'd be wearing jeans or doing a festive rap.

She returned to Jeff with two coffees.

"Where have you been ?".

"You don't think that turkey will cook itself ?".

"I thought it might be self-basting".

"Shut up you lazy sod. You can prepare the vegetables".

"Whatever".

Both could hardly believe their luck, it was such a change

from all the previous years of family squabbles - nothing much demanded apart from eating, drinking and frequent sex.

"I wonder if my dad got a mobile phone ?".

"Just a satsuma and some nuts I'd expect".

"I suppose we'll have to visit the parents at some point".

"Let's not think about it now, you'll put me off dinner".

As Et dozed off, Jeff watched a light flurry of snow through the bedroom window. He looked back at her peaceful face on the pillow, thinking again of all the good times they'd had over the year. He got up, and looked down at the stream with tiny ice floes clinging to muddy banks. Snow was starting to settle on the road, and the occasional car made little impression on the white surface.

"Et, it's getting thicker".

She slept like an ice princess, that Jeff fantasised only he could wake - a fantasy that was almost true, almost perfect, as long as he did nothing really stupid in the months and years to come.

He knew that his mum and dad must have started something like this, but at what point did all turn sour, how did they take the wrong road ? Whatever happened Jeff was determined not to end up taking pictures up strangers skirts - he couldn't face becoming his dad.

"What are you thinking ?".

"Just looking at the snow".

"How thick is it ?".

"An inch or so".

"We'll have to get dinner sorted".

"Lovely sprouts. But did you know fine words butter no parsnips ?".

"You're talking crap again ! That doesn't apply to our roast vegetables anyway".

Jeff went to the kitchen to do his bit with the peeler, while sipping Guinness Foreign Extra Stout from a large glass. It tasted nothing like the draught creamy brew served at the Little Angel - this was deep-roasted, almost burnt. While indulging himself he hoped Et wouldn't intrude, after all a man likes to get on with the job, whether it be peeling spuds or chiselling a lump of wood in the shed.

Snow was still falling, and he could hear kids going past the cottage pulling sledges. Jeff realised it was only a few years before that he'd done the same with mates from school. Now any such trip would be in the more sophisticated company of Et, unless Dave called round on his motorbike (not likely in snow).

"The power had better stay on", said Et, coming to check the bird.

"I'm sure it will".

"I've never cooked a turkey before".

"You're kidding, you mean you're a poultry virgin ?".

"No.......I stuffed a chicken once".

"It smells great anyway".

"You can't beat a local bird".

"I'd have to agree with that".

It made him happy to watch her enjoying the role of mother, taking care of all the details, whether it be mixing stuffing, preparing gravy, bread sauce or cranberry jelly - just as Et had watched and helped her mum over the years.

"Get the spuds in then, not long to go".

"Are there any chipolatas ?".

"Don't worry, baby Lincolnshire sausages. Now you can sod off for a bit and let me get on with it".

"OK, I'm going".

26

Following the hearty meal Et was fast asleep in front of the fire, and Jeff dozed in and out of dreams. Did the Queen really say that hit men hired by her were responsible for the death of Diana, Princess of Wales ? All so Charles could marry an old bag. A somewhat surprising Christmas speech.

Reality returned with a knock on the door - Roger and Paul were standing in the snow, laden with festive fayre.

"Et, wake up ! It's those puffs".

Jeff was compelled to answer the door himself, as Et came round too slowly, and it was too late to hide.

"Now then Jeff ! Thought we'd pop round with a few offerings".

"Very nice, come in", he muttered.

"Hope we're not disturbing anything. Did you see the Queen's speech ? Very different", said Roger.

"Sit down, please", invited Et.

"It must be four inches thick out there", said Paul.

"I'll make some tea", suggested Jeff.

"Try something stronger", said Roger, producing a bottle of port.

"Four glasses then", said Et.

Jeff looked out of the window at the dark road covered in snow, wishing he could follow the silent call to the high Wold.

"I think it's stopped for now", Paul said.

He didn't turn round, just continued looking at the changed world beyond.

"Don't be rude Jeff, we've got guests".

"Sorry, I was just looking at the snow".

"What have you two been doing over Christmas ?", asked Et.

"Lots of drinking and telly. Wasn't the power cut a hoot ?", laughed Paul.

"Hilarious", Jeff replied in a sarcastic tone.

"You've got the place looking lovely", complimented Roger.

"Nice and cosy", said Et.

"Cheers then !", Roger said loudly.

All four raised and brought glasses together.

"At least the pub's open again", said Paul, breaking the silence.

"No sign of the landlord though !", replied Roger.

Et went to the kitchen and brought back a bowl of cheese footballs and some salted peanuts.

"It set me thinking, seeing the Queen's speech. Do you know who changed my life for the better ?", Paul fixed his gaze on Jeff.

"No, but I bet you're going to tell me".

"Sarah Ferguson, Duchess of York".

"Amazing", said Jeff.

"The way she overcame her lack of self-esteem, well......it's inspiring".

"I don't find Budgie the Helicopter books on a par with The Little Prince, for example", Et chipped in.

"The Duchess had to sit on the end of her bed and face the demons that made her eat or spend uncontrollably. She's helped me no end with my addiction to large sausages and sauerkraut".

"Yes, he has changed", confirmed Roger.

"You can't beat a cheese football", said Jeff.

"Very popular in our youth", Paul agreed.

It started to snow again, and Jeff watched the thick flakes, wishing he could escape, even though the two chaps didn't seem as bad as he first thought all those months ago at Wold House.

"I hope the power stays on".

"Don't worry Et, you can always come to us - we've got a back-up generator", offered Roger.

"We'll manage", said Jeff.

27

The next morning Jeff woke first and went straight to look out of the window. He was excited to see the snow was now a couple of feet thick. Rather than wake Et, which was his first thought, he decided to go for a short walk in the icy wilderness.

First he had some tea and toast, then made sure the fire wasn't about to go out, then looked for some long socks and wellies. It was only 8:15 and most people were still in bed, and most weren't at work anyway because of Christmas and New Year. Not that any cars would be driven out of the village, as all four routes were impassable.

As he walked away from home it was easy to imagine himself an intrepid explorer - the first human to discover this new world without footprints. And it was a totally new world, because familiar bumps and landmarks had been lost or completely transformed by the significant snowfall. Jeff wasn't sure, but he thought it was the deepest snow that had fallen in his short lifetime.

"Global warming my arse !", he muttered.

It was fairly easy walking along the flat lane that led to the Wold itself, by the beck mostly hidden under ice and snow. So many times he'd taken this route, but never in such extreme wintry conditions. He hadn't even bothered to tell Et where he was going or for how long, but Jeff felt sure it would be OK if he didn't go far.

Once he climbed the gate and started up the lower slopes it became impossible to make decent progress. Snow was over welly tops, and every few yards he fell over and laughed loudly.

Jeff wished he had woken Et, because they could have had great fun rolling about. Before he met her solitude seemed a more natural state, but now he'd been spoilt by her vivacious company.

So he turned his back on the hills that seemed like great pillows of soft ice making nature and the unnatural motor car silent - the only sound being his own feet slipping home on the rough path made a short time before.

"You must be mad going out in this".

"I didn't get far".

"What if you'd twisted an ankle ?".

"It's the Yorkshire Wolds, not the bloody Himalayas !".

"You should have woken me".

"But you looked so sweet".

"Get some more coal luv, I'll put the kettle on".

Jeff had to go out again, and as he carried the fuel back flakes began to fall.

"Bloody hell, we could be stuck for ages", Et worried.

"Don't start again, we've got plenty of food. It's wonderful just to experience life in another dimension - so what if we can't get to the shops for a few days !?".

"You're usually in a different world anyway. It's the rest of us that deserve some magic".

"Fine, I'm sure you can forget the January sales that have already started in December".

"But I need some new clothes".

"Your wardrobe is full of outfits that are never worn !".

"I'm still growing".

"So am I, but I'm not sure it's upwards".

28

It didn't snow any more after that, but the roads were unusable for days, and drifts refused to budge from verges and hedgerows. When they walked up to the Little Angel on New Year's Eve the path was polished and treacherous.

"Fuckin' hell ! I'm gonna break a leg here".

"Hold on to me", said Et.

"We'll both go down !".

"Just go slowly".

They could hear the music from a long way off, it seemed like Christmas Eve all over again.

"Maybe I won't stay long".

"Are you mad ? It's New Year's Eve !", Jeff replied.

"I don't know if I can stand the noise after the quiet time we've had".

"You'll get into it luv".

Jeff pushed open the door to a rowdy bar, saying hello to the usual crowd, including many of the folk he'd grown up with. Julie was working hard behind the bar and looked reasonably happy.

"Hi Jeff !".

"Now then Dave, fancy seeing you here".

"I'll get you both a drink".

"Wouldn't say no".

Jeff found a slightly quieter table in the snug, and Et did her best to cheer up. Suddenly the bar went quiet.

"What's happening ?", wondered Dave.

"No idea", said Et.

Jeff went to have a look, and was stunned to see Pete standing near the door with a packed bar of villagers staring at him with real venom. He rushed back to the snug.

"What's going on ?!".

"You won't believe who's just come in".

"Nelson Mandela ? Kylie Minogue ?", said Dave.

"It's only Pete !".

"Jesus Christ !", said Et.

"Fuckin' hell !", said Dave.

Julie stood in a state of shock for what felt like ages, and all the clientele were silent waiting for something to happen. Then she screamed and ran towards the stairs.

Sonia, the village ex-nun went towards Pete:

"I think you'd better piss-off before it turns nasty".

"I'm not going anywhere".

Next up was the farmer from down Leppington Lane, who started to push Pete towards the door. Shouts of 'fuck off' and 'get out' were heard from the angry throng. Several locals then joined in the push, and the former landlord was at last forced into the car park.

"Get back to your tart !", the ex-nun shouted.

Et went upstairs to see if she could comfort Julie. Dave went to get some more drinks from the bar. Gradually noise returned to the Little Angel, as all were passionately discussing the rights and wrongs of the situation.

Julie was crying, and Et did her best to bring some comfort.

"Why in God's name did he come back tonight of all nights ?".

"I don't know", said Et.

"Has he gone ?".

"Chucked out".

"That's something, I don't ever want to see him".

"You don't have to".

"Do you think he's finished with her ?".

"Maybe, I don't know".

"But why come back tonight ?".

Et could offer no answers, but tried to hold Julie as tightly as possible to give some reassurance.

"Shall I close the pub ?".

"No, there'd be a riot".

"OK".

"Anyway, I'm not letting that bastard get me down".

"That's the spirit".

Downstairs the music was back on and beer flowing, a happy atmosphere returned as midnight approached. Et rejoined Jeff and Dave - Julie promised to come down in a little while.

"How is she ?", Jeff asked.

"Not too bad, considering".

"I can't believe he came back tonight", said Dave.

"Here, have a drink luv".

"Yea, I need it. That poor woman".

Et hadn't been relishing their night out, and she certainly didn't imagine this would happen. She felt utterly exhausted, and unable to join in the celebrations.

"I'm going home".

"I'll just get my coat".

"No, you stay with Dave".

"He'll be alright, that lass over there has been hot for him all night".

So the two of them slipped out the side door at eleven o'clock, into the car park still thick with frozen snow. They didn't chat much on the way back, but neither was uncomfortable with silence - just glad to be walking home together.

The fire had nearly burnt out in the ash-choked grate, and Jeff knelt down to give it a good poke.

"Soon have it going", he said.

As if the rising flames could somehow repair any sadness at the Little Angel, but more importantly raise the spirits of his lovely, tired girl.

"I'll get some whisky".

Et went to the kitchen, leaving Jeff to stare into the low fire with its ever-changing shape. Only thirty minutes to a new year, not that either of them believed that December 31st was any more significant than April 25th or August 9th or September 8th.

"I needed that. Sorry to drag you home again", Et said.

"I suppose we can thank my dad for this booze, if nothing else".

He looked into her large, sad eyes, no less mysterious than the rising flames he was lost in a little earlier.

"I love you".

"Love you too", she replied, touching his arm.

"Julie will be alright".

"I'm not so sure. It was a real shock for her seeing him tonight".

Jeff felt it would not be easy to bring Et back to cheerfulness, so he filled her glass and then his own with the powerful liquor. When he looked at the clock a while later it showed 12:23 - the new year had come unnoticed.

29

The return to work after the festive break was particularly painful for Jeff, wrenched from his beloved countryside into a harsh world of forms and numbers. It was no fun travelling there either these icy mornings - once or twice he nearly lost the back wheel of his scooter. He decided it must be worth the effort though, if money generated kept them together at Beck Cottage.

At least there was his mature, lady friend - Emily, to maintain some sanity in the dull, unfriendly office. She looked just as attractive and serene as always when they met in the tea room.

"Good break ?", she asked, smiling.

"Plenty of snow".

"Not much fun coming back".

"You can say that again".

"I stayed in a cottage in Coverdale with a friend".

Jeff wondered if that was a girlfriend or boyfriend, sexual or platonic - she didn't talk much about her private life, but was always interested in his relationship with Et.

"Your first Christmas together".

"Mostly just the two of us".

"That's how it should be at your age".

As usual he couldn't ignore the sweet shape of her breasts, but tried not to make it obvious. What was the difference between admiring a beautiful view in the Wolds and staring at a lovely woman ? The hills aren't likely to say 'stop looking at my tits !'.

"I suppose we'll have to do some work - see you later".

"See you later", said Jeff.

As he looked up from the flickering computer screen, Jeff scanned all the miserable faces of dear colleagues. Maybe none of them were serious dreamers like himself, but all had escaped for two weeks from the daily grind and were finding working reality a problem. Even Marjorie (nicknamed 'the hyena'), who normally laughed in a way that brought the atmosphere of Africa right into the office, seemed rather subdued.

It wasn't long before young Kelly came round to collect money for the lottery syndicate:

"Same numbers Jeff ?".

"No, I'll choose some new ones".

He fished into a dog-eared brown envelope for the little scraps of numbered paper, and Kelly wrote them down.

"Maybe we won't be back at work long !", she said.

Jeff wished this could be true, but the chances of winning more than ten quid were very, very slim.

He returned to entering numbers on the computer, but the days of getting up late and going to bed late had taken their toll. Two hours to lunch, and he wondered how it was possible to stay awake, let alone do some work without making mistakes.

Every so often he thought about Et beavering away at the hotel, and realised that office life could be pretty easy if you knew how to work the system. Plenty of little chats, lots of trips to the bog, off to the tea room, an excursion to collect some more paper that isn't really needed. He'd heard about these call centres though, where all your activity is monitored and you can't go to the bog, and one place the boss made people wear nappies to save time away from answering phones. These jobs were moving to India now, where they pay graduates a pittance to give information about a remote England they don't know.

The sky was typically grey and cold for January; even so Jeff would much rather have been climbing up the Wold, listening to the loud beck hurtling to the river, carrying so much rain, ever so much rain and melted snow.

He was getting his scooter from the car park at 4:30 when Emily came up:

"I'm glad I've got a warm car, I don't envy you on that motorbike".

"Not much fun at this time of year".

"Do you fancy calling in at my place for a cuppa ?".

"Where do you live ?".

"It's on your way home, in Norton".

"Well.......I should get back".

"Go on, a few minutes won't hurt - you can follow my car".

Emily had a lovely place overlooking the river, though the deep water was rather brown and uninviting in winter. Her flat made the sparse decoration of Beck Cottage seem rather shabby in Jeff's mind. He didn't want to appear foolish by asking her what the style was, but guessed Moroccan from the make-over programmes Et liked to watch.

"Make yourself comfortable, I'll put the kettle on".

He felt uneasy, as Emily was nearly as old as his mum, and he didn't really know what to say. The feeling got worse when she returned in a short dressing gown that was hardly fastened at the front.

"Tea won't be long".

"I'll have to go soon".

"Relax".

He couldn't help noticing the exposure of breast was even greater than the office, but daren't let his gaze linger for more than a second. She went to the kitchen and Jeff wondered how to make an escape, but then reasoned that it would be silly to run off.

"Here we are".

She brought the tray in and sat close to him on the sofa. Now Jeff could clearly see she wasn't wearing any knickers, as her thick dark bush was clearly visible.

"I'll have to go".

"No need".

Emily stood up and pulled open the gown, revealing her trim body only a few inches from his face.

"What do you think ?".

"I've got to go, really".

"It's alright, we're just good friends".

Jeff was in a state of shock, and as he stood up to make for the exit knocked over the coffee table.

"I'm sorry", he said, rushing towards the door.

30

After fleeing the scene of no crime (at least on his part) Jeff was pleased to find that Et hadn't got back to Beck Cottage, allowing precious time to gain composure. He didn't think there was any point in upsetting her by telling the story of how they take afternoon tea in Norton. Jeff was reasonably satisfied that his actions had been above board, and couldn't be responsible for what might be going on in the subconscious mind.

He opened a Guinness Foreign Extra Stout to steady frayed nerves, trying to concentrate only on the behaviour of the dark liquid that had been freed like a genie from the brown bottle. Jeff was very much in favour of sharing everything with his lover, but guessed that such an episode would trouble her mind for years to come.

He slumped in a chair with eyes closed, flashes of Emily's naked flesh kept invading his weary brain. Out of the window a hail shower grew louder, as it bounced off the road and pavement. The fire that burned low in the grate didn't bring its usual comfort - his mind was bursting with conflicting emotion that must be kept from Et at all costs.

"Sorry I'm late".

"It's OK, I haven't been back long myself".

"Started on the drink already !".

"It's very stressful going back to work".

"You should try doing my job - changing beds, cleaning toilets, washing up, serving meals".

"Healthier than sitting in a chair all day staring at a computer".

"Get me a beer please luv, I'm jiggered".

Jeff went to the kitchen, happy to take on any routine task that might avoid contemplating the disturbing events of earlier. When he returned Et was sat in front of the fire warming her hands and toes.

"So how was it, your first day back ?".

"Very tiring. And you ?".

"The same. I'll be old before my time if I stay at that hotel".

He sat down and put his arm round her waist, planting a tender kiss on her chilly cheek.

"Blimey, you are cold".

"Hold me tighter then".

"I don't want to crush you".

"You go ahead and crush".

Jeff felt tears welling as he struggled to blot out Emily's fragrant body; he pulled Et closer, trying desperately to remain in the present with the girl he loved so deeply. For now the hail had turned to icy rain beating on the window sills of the cottage; as long as he held her tightly Jeff felt safe from known and unknown threats approaching from the outer world.

"I'll make something to eat", said Et.

"A thick stew with dumplings, to combat this bitter weather ?".

"You'll be lucky ! What about a microwave curry ?".

"Whatever. Bring me another drink while you're there".

"What did your last slave die of ?".

"My mother is still alive and well and living with a pervert !".

Jeff poked the fire half-heartedly, wondering how he'd overcome the awkwardness of facing Emily at work. It would be difficult to speak to her in the same way having seen most of her awe-inspiring flesh.

"Chicken Tikka or Jalfrezi ?", Et shouted.

"Jalfrezi".

"Guinness or lager ?".

If they could just keep to everyday discussions about food and drink, Jeff felt sure other matters would gradually recede into the background and eventually be forgotten. No doubt Et had some things she chose to keep to herself, simply to protect their still youthful relationship. Some people say you shouldn't hide anything from a partner, but total openness felt much too risky now - maybe he'd tell her when they were sixty-five, and both could have a really good laugh at the follies of those early days.

31

Because of his part-time status it was a relief to Jeff that the day following the ordeal by nudity was a free day, and he felt the need to get away from familiar surroundings altogether. When Et had gone to the hotel he started the longish walk to the top road for a bus to the seaside resort of Bridlington.

He was pleased to see some patches of blue in the sky - the radio weather promised sun on the coast with a chill wind from Scandinavia. The ride over the high wolds and down to the sea was one he'd taken many times with family and more recently with Et - Jeff found himself nodding-off as the bus made good progress on fairly quiet roads.

Bridlington always felt rather run-down in parts compared to Scarborough and Whitby, though millions had been spent on revitalising the long seaside promenades. Away from the immediate town centre, side streets of enormous red-brick houses hinted at a lost prosperity - now either cheap B&B's or very sad looking bedsits.

Jeff walked straight from the bus station to the harbour, keen to get an early taste of genuine Yorkshire seaside life - not the shop chains that can be found in any British town or city. He wandered close to the brown water, watching gulls and fishing boats bobbing on the high tide. As it was mid-week the town was much less busy than weekends, that even in winter could be quite lively with visitors from Hull or Leeds.

Thoughts of Et and Emily kept coming into his mind, but he didn't find it too difficult to dismiss sharp memories of the dressing gown incident, being away from familiar haunts. Here it was amusement arcades - some were open, though the mini-rollercoaster and giant log flume stayed wrapped-up till late spring.

He walked north in the direction of Sewerby, looking down

on the sandy beach that became more and more pebbled. There were some old folk walking dogs near the gentle waves, and a man with a metal detector hoping for that one big find to make retirement more comfortable.

Jeff felt the wind penetrate his jacket, and started to think of fish and chips back at the harbour, he turned towards the town framed by a startling blue sky.

"One of each please".

"Scraps with that luv ?", the stout, red-faced lady asked.

"Yes please".

She shovelled a heap of dark golden batter fragments on top of cod and chips.

"Lovely day", she smiled.

"Yes".

His mate Dave had said that somebody they knew went into a chippy and asked for one of each. Instead of being served the required fish and chips they were given one of each item from the entire menu. Jeff didn't really believe the story, though he could imagine a tray piled high with chips, fish, sausage, mushy peas, meat pie, fish cake, pickled egg..........

He sat on a seat in the shelter of a high wall and began to eat, trying not to attract the attention of gulls that were the size of small children. In many ways not much had changed since the family holidays that had been both painful and joyous. The fishing boats looked the same, and the large pleasure cruiser they'd often been on towards Flamborough was identical, except for yet another coat of white paint to hide serious rust.

Jeff looked south along the miles of lovely sand stretching towards Spurn, remembering all the sand castles they'd built, the ice creams dropped, and pop spilt. He thought about his dad and the mildly perverse activities that now occupied this man, once the centre of an occasionally magical childhood.

But it was not summer, and the January beach was virtually

deserted. Instead of great chalk cliffs to the north that seemed to liberate all the wolds into relentless sea, the south was low crumbling mud, villages disappearing into chocolate waves.

Back in the town centre he had a choice of coffee bars that had somehow survived unchanged from the fifties and sixties - the kind of places you'd get hot drinks in a glass rather than a cup. Jeff chose one that overlooked the south beach, and he sat for an hour watching waves in a gigantic mirror. The other customers were entirely pensioners, feasting on fake Italian ice cream with squirty UHT cream on top.

By 3:30 the sun had lost its power and the mirror let go of the sea, making the cafe cramped again with dog-eared decor. He walked back to the bus station, hoping for a short wait, a little snooze over rolling hills, then back home with Et.

32

When Jeff got back to Beck Cottage he was surprised to find it deserted, and a barely legible note from Et on the table: 'Gone to pub. Ladies Night !'.

"Fuckin' Ladies Night", he grumbled.

His mood was not improved by finding the fire nearly dead in the grate.

"Bloody hell !", he shouted at the empty room.

Visions of a cosy night on the couch with Et had been shattered by the magnetism of a male stripper. She had mentioned something about trying to cheer Julie up following the unexpected visit of her runaway husband, but he never imagined she'd actually go.

He grabbed a beer, and with a little attention the fire began to climb and brighten their small lounge. Jeff realised how dependent he'd become on the company of Et, and had no idea what to do with himself.

The Internet provided brief amusement, but he quickly found that it was an empty experience without a specific task to complete, like buy a CD or send an email. When he first switched on there were 17 emails waiting, all of which were junk and mainly relating to sex.

As always all were selected and deleted; presumably some people were stupid enough to open this type of thing, or the spammers wouldn't bother.

Naturally he was tempted to try the I Ching, but felt guilty because of happiness with Et (if happy why meddle), and her very low opinion of astrology and other 'dark arts'.

"If she can watch a bloke take his kit off, why shouldn't I do my thing", he muttered at the screen.

So now he had to come up with a valid question, nothing frivolous that might incur the wrath of unknown forces. Jeff typed: 'What is likely to happen about work ?', and then repeated the question in his mind several times. After clicking the button he waited for the slow computer to respond. Then he heard the door latch.

"Fuckin' hell !".

Et was back already.

"Jeff ?".

"Just coming".

He switched the computer off at the wall socket.

"What are you up to ?", she asked affectionately.

"Waiting for you darling. Did you see his willy ?".

"No, I left just before he removed the black satin posing pouch".

"It's disgusting, degrading men like that !".

"The ladies seemed to enjoy it, though Julie's still depressed".

Jeff fetched some beers and joined Et in front of the fire.

"How was Brid. then ?".

"Good. We'll have to go together when it warms up".

"When will that be ?".

"June or July".

"Did you miss me today ?".

"Why would I ?".

"Because you love me".

Jeff leaned over and kissed her tenderly, just to re-affirm what she already knew. The fire burned well, they were back together in their borrowed cottage, and the nasty world was locked out behind a heavy, oak door.

"Both at work tomorrow".

"Great", sighed Jeff.

He started to worry about how things would go with Emily.

"I'm going to bed".

"OK, I won't be long", he replied.

He went to the kitchen and poured a large glass of Black Bush Irish Whiskey, then settled back in front of the fire. Tears started to roll down his warm face, tears he could hardly explain.

33

Jeff was astounded by Emily's behaviour when he returned to the dreaded office - she was exactly the same, as if she'd never put all her most valuable assets on show. He wondered why his last few days had been tainted by worry, when this woman clearly didn't give a toss.

"Morning Jeff", she said cheerily.

"Morning".

"You're looking well".

"I am ?".

He sat at the computer wondering if any colleagues had been invited to her flat, and if one or two had leapt at the chance of feasting on those lovely breasts and moist cunt.

"Got enough to do ?", said the section manager.

"Plenty", Jeff replied.

"I'd like to see all those reports entered by close of play".

"Right".

As soon as the boss had gone Jeff went to get a cuppa and settled back at his desk gazing out at an unusually blue sky. It was much more in keeping with Health and Safety to stare at the sky rather than a PC. He wondered how Et was getting on at the hotel - probably clearing away breakfasts now, scraping fatty bacon rind and bits of fried egg into the bin.

It was a big relief that Emily was behaving 'normally', and for a fleeting moment he thought office life wasn't too bad. There was no denying she had a great figure, and if he hadn't been totally committed to Et - who knows ?!

Following an afternoon of almost nodding off, he made sure that Emily left a long time before himself to avoid any mis-understandings in the car park. It was getting slowly lighter in the evenings, nothing spectacular, but there were some divine colours as he looked west towards York.

It was mild days like these when he began to re-discover the pleasures of riding a motorbike, after the dark and icy months that hadn't entirely passed, yet spring was surely hinted at - he could almost see daffodils on long green verges.

The cottage lights told him Et was home, and as the door opened a lovely smell came from the kitchen, reminiscent of so many years at home when his mum would prepare stew and dumplings or Sunday roast.

"Smells good".

"Your favourite".

"It can't be chilli, chips and cheese ?!".

"No, a thick beef stew with carrots and peas".

"Are you trying to fatten me up ?".

"The ale's doing a good job of that already".

"What do you mean ? I've got the body of a young man".

"A lazy sod, more like".

Jeff didn't mind cooking, but it was good to be waited on occasionally, feeling some kind of continuity from the simple family lives they'd both known. Rabbits and pheasants were always abundant as they were growing up, though he was a little wary of finding dead creatures hanging in the shed. A cleanly prepared joint from the supermarket could be less challenging for a sensitive soul.

"What do you want to drink with it ?".

"Shall we try that bottle of red wine the puffs brought ?".

"Don't be so unpleasant, they were very good to you".

"Suppose you're right, as always".

"Women usually are".

Jeff didn't bother to dignify this remark with a reply, instead poked the fire with a greater ferocity than usual. He began to think how far they'd come since he was living at Wold House, the days when it was necessary to sneak into Et's, trying not to tread on the creaky stairs. Their happiness scared him, or at least the possibility of it all disappearing overnight like snow washed away by rain.

34

It had been quite a tough winter at the foot of the Wold, maybe nothing compared with when his dad was little (or so the old man claimed), but here they were stuck at home again after a heavy band of snow moved down from Scotland. Jeff looked at the snowman across the road that kids had dressed with a red cap, and the usual carrot and coals. A significant fall overnight had been followed by a few blizzards during the day, that had finally forced the kids inside after a splendid day with the school closed.

"They won't be happy at the hotel, all these days I've had off", fretted Et.

"What can you do ? It would be silly to try and get there on these roads".

"You know what that manager's like - a real cunt !".

"He'd better not show his face in the Little Angel".

"He doesn't drink".

"There you go then, he's not normal".

"He assaulted one lass in a guest bedroom - tore her dress".

"I'll fuckin' kill him if he goes near you".

"Don't worry, I know a few karate moves myself".

Jeff was more relaxed about his own further absence as they had a clear policy on 'acts of God', or extreme weather. Some neighbours had driven or slid to work in the big town, but he was happy to take the AA radio warnings literally and only make essential journeys - like to the Little Angel.

"We'll be running out of logs and coal at this rate".

"You sound just like your mother", Jeff laughed.

"Someone has to do the worrying - I know you won't bother".

"It's me who always lights the bloody thing".

"Men are always poking at something".

"Now you sound like my mother !".

The bushes outside were trembling in the late afternoon as more flakes of snow swirled above them, it was hard to tell which way the wind was blowing. When he'd been to the coal bunker it felt like minus-ten, rather than the zero predicted. And the little beck had disappeared completely under ice and a heap of white stuff.

"Make another pot of tea luv".

"You'll be wetting yourself", said Jeff.

"And toasted teacakes with the real butter - not marg.".

"Whatever you say dear".

The snow was now blowing horizontally from the north, and the poor snowman's cap was turning from red to white. As he boiled the kettle Jeff prayed the power wouldn't go off, he wasn't sure if they had a spare canister for the camping stove. Because neither of them had expected to be at home, it felt better than an ordinary day off - a gift from above.

"You can't beat a strong cuppa and some hot teacakes".

"I won't argue with you", Jeff replied.

"You wouldn't dare".

"I'll rip your dress off in an instant".

"I'll kick you in the balls".

"I'll tear off all your clothes and shove you out in the snow drift".

"But my nipples will go all hard".

As darkness came they wondered if the next morning would force them out the door and into the world of work - it didn't feel like the weather would suddenly turn mild, quite the reverse. What could they do but crack open another bottle from their diminishing stock of alcohol ? It might do nothing scientifically or medically to keep the body warm, but the important thing was it felt like a positive effect.

The next morning Jeff got up at six, mentally resigned to working despite severe overnight ice and drifting snow. When it was light he wandered round the village still entirely white, to check if the roads were passable. At the bottom of the hill from

Acklam a car had run into the hedge. He watched a Renault Clio snaking up the steep hill near the Little Angel. The main road to the big town was still dangerous, and the steep hill onto Wold top was like a ski-jumping descent.

"What a shame", he said to himself.

Back at the cottage Et was wandering about in her tatty dressing gown.

"Well ?".

"Not a chance of getting out today".

"I'll have to try and walk".

"Don't be silly".

"I'll get the sack".

"It's just too icy", insisted Jeff.

Et wasn't happy at being cooped-up another day, they couldn't even get to a shop to buy bread and milk. She hated the hotel job, but as long as the cash was flowing they could continue their independent life. To go back and live with parents now would be unbearable, and she thought that such a backward step would ruin their relationship for good.

The morning sky was such a lovely blue that Jeff did feel slightly guilty about missing work, but he'd checked the roads carefully and there was just no way out. Colleagues that lived close to the office would doubtless be complaining, though they had the advantage of being close to amenities.

"We can take the sledge out later".

"Maybe", said Et sulking.

"There's no point being miserable".

She knew that he was right, though decided not to give in to a happy mood until at least 10:30.

35

"I'm off for a walk, are you coming ?".

"No, it's too cold".

"Fine, I'll see you later".

"Where are you going ?".

It was too late as Jeff was already outside and on his way towards Thixendale. If Et was determined to be miserable, he'd decided to get out in the snow and clear his mind. She felt sad now he'd left so abruptly, but they could make it up later.

As usual Jeff was well-equipped for the conditions, but as he got up to the Wold top drifts were several feet thick. The sky was still brilliant blue and the wind had dropped from the night before. He looked down towards the big town, across rolling and then flat fields of white.

On ordinary days cars and Land Rovers would be speeding along the ridge, but it was so quiet up there, not even another rambler had ventured out. He dropped down off the road towards a steep-sided valley where the walking was very difficult, Jeff began to wonder if his idea of making Thixendale and a meal at the cafe had been a big mistake.

Et wasn't concerned as she looked out at the sunny sky, she knew he'd walked the hills for years in all kinds of weather. A chance to get the vacuum cleaner out, move furniture, and vent frustration into a vigorous domestic purification ritual. When Jeff returned she could prepare a hot tea, and they could watch some nonsense on telly.

He slipped and started to roll over and over, eventually coming to a halt in some soft snow fifty-feet below. When he tried to stand up his right ankle was too painful to take any weight, and he fell back unable to move. It was about three miles home and another four to Thixendale; there hadn't been any point bringing a mobile as no reception was possible.

"Hello !", he shouted into the emptiness.

Jeff knew there would be nobody around, he hadn't even seen a sheep on the journey. It was extremely cold in the steep valley bottom, and he began to feel more and more pessimistic about the situation. Et might start to get worried after dark, but that was seven hours away, and even if they were prepared to start a search at night it would be many hours later before help arrived.

He tried to stand again, but it was hopeless:

"Arghhhhh !!!", his scream rang round the icy slopes.

Toes and fingers were very cold already, snow had forced its way up his back and trouser legs in the fall. He started to think about Et, and warm tears rolled down frozen cheeks. A noise startled him, but as he strained to catch sight of the source it became obvious that a pheasant or pheasants had broken cover - startled by an imaginary shooting party.

"Et !", he yelled hopelessly.

Maybe the closeness they'd developed would mean that she could hear a voice in her mind, maybe just a vague feeling of doubt that everything wasn't quite right.

Wold